THE HOAX

Sophie Masson was born in Indonesia of French parents, moved to Australia in 1963 and grew up in Sydney. She now lives in Invergowrie, New South Wales, with her husband and three children, and writes for both adults and children. She is also a contributor to *Quadrant*, the *Australian* and the *Guardian Weekly*.

Also by Sophie Masson

For adults
The House in the Rainforest

For children
The Opera Club
The Cousin from France
Winter in France
The Secret
Family Business
Birds of a Feather
Illusion
The First Day
Carabas
The Gifting
The Sun is Rising

THE HOAX

SOPHIE MASSON

MINERVA

A Minerva book
published by
Random House Australia Pty Ltd
20 Alfred Street, Milsons Point, NSW 2061
http://www.randomhouse.com.au

Sydney New York Toronto
London Auckland Johannesburg

First published 1997

Copyright © Sophie Masson 1997

All rights reserved. Without limiting the rights under copyright above, no part of this publication may be reproduced, stored in or introduced into a retrieval system, or transmitted in any form or by any means (electronic, mechanical, photocopying, recording or otherwise), without the prior written permission of both the copyright owner and the publisher.

All characters and events in this book are fictitious and any resemblance to real organisations or real persons, living or dead, is purely coincidental.

Typeset in Australia by Emtype Desktop Publishing Pty Ltd
Printed and bound in Australia by Griffin Press

National Library of Australia
cataloguing-in-publication data:

Masson, Sophie, 1959– .
The hoax.

ISBN 1 86330 542 4.

Title.

A823.3

10 9 8 7 6 5 4 3 2 1

Ce voyageur ailé, comme il est gauche et veule!
Lui, naguère si beau, qu'il est comique et laid!
L'un agace son bec avec un brûle-gueule,
L'autre mime, en boitant, l'infirme qui volait!

'L'Albatros', Charles Baudelaire

He is awkward and weak now, who once ruled the air!
Comically ugly, yet once past compare!
Tormented with fire by one in the crew,
While another mimes, limping, he who once flew!

translation by Sophie Masson

contents

Part One

Once
1

Part Two

Before
75

Part Three

The Abyss
129

Acknowledgments
254

Bibliography
255

Part 1

ONCE

one

This was rag-and-bone country: high cold country of gaunt spur and broken curve, thinly clothed with pale native grasses. Only the sky was lavish, sumptuously billowing with gold and crimson and pink in the west, edged with the lilac of advancing night. The train passed through this stern landscape with a waddle and a swagger, disturbing the animals that had come down to eat the few pockets of green grass near the tracks. Through the windows, Alex could see them fleeing up the hills from the noise of the train's passage, and the sight made him smile. Bob-tailed rabbits, pale kangaroos, lumbering cattle, rictus-baring foxes, skeltering sheep—all fleeing headlong, without dignity, as if they had been caught unawares.

He hadn't been up this way for so long. It was like discovering the country all over again. He carefully stored the pictures of it all in his head, because then their calm beauty would help him, later. Going up to see Julius was something he had been putting off for a long time. Only Isabelle understood his reluctance; everyone else he knew, at work, in their circle of friends, was filled with admiration, with envy. *What an interesting life he's had! What marvellous things he writes, so clear, so beautiful! What a wonderful childhood you must have had, growing up with Julius Newton!* Even the children agitated to see him, for Julius treated them as favoured adults, handing out unsuitable presents, buying them treats of the kind Alex and Isabelle could never afford and so did not approve.

But Roxane was back, and it was the old man's seventieth birthday, and there was no escaping it. He had received what could only be called a summons, in his uncle's soft rounded writing. 'My dear Alex,' Julius had written, 'it is a long time since we saw you, and as my three-score-years-and-ten approaches, I feel the need for familiar people around me. I know family life and your work are pressing, but do you think you could see your way to coming here for a few days?'

Julius somehow always managed to make Alex feel as if he were in the wrong, to suggest that Alex's concerns were trifling, his life diminished. He had never understood why Alex would not follow up the contacts he, Julius, provided for him; did not understand why his nephew had chosen to become a lowly schoolteacher; why when he finally began to write books he had written for children. Alex had said this to Isabelle, and she had laughed, said he read too much into simple words; but then Julius was an in-law for her, not immediate family. It was easier to be detached then. And besides, she could always pretend she didn't fully understand English; could always take refuge in the preconceptions even Julius might have of her because of her French accent.

At the end of the letter, his uncle had written, 'Your Aunt Roxane will also be glad to see you.' What? Roxane back? That was news indeed. Isabelle thought it astonishing that Roxane hadn't contacted him, but Alex knew his aunt. She would simply not have wanted to intrude, not being sure of her welcome. But how typical of Julius to assume that Alex somehow must have been aware of Roxane's return, simply because he was.

Isabelle had said, with a sideways glance at her husband, that she and the children would stay in Sydney, for Alex, she suggested, would need time to renew the bonds. She thought that family always won through in the end, for so it had been in her family.

Of course, she had never known Roxane, hardly even through Alex's memories. On the phone Julius had asked politely, charmingly, as he always did, after Isabelle's health and the children's, and Alex had gabbled that Isabelle couldn't make it, because her cousin was over for a holiday and besides he supposed the house wouldn't have been geared towards children. He smiled to himself. As if Julius ever noticed when you made excuses! It had always been thus, for as far back as Alex could remember.

Julius had begun to make his reputation as a biographer of composers in the decade after the Second World War. His first book, on Beethoven, had burst onto the scene in a kind of sulphurous blaze, creating an immense *succès de scandale*. For it combined the elegant, cool style for which Julius was now famous with a powerful, rather disturbing thesis about the composer's real self. Julius' subsequent books had been much praised, though not as fiercely discussed, but his place in the literary scene was secure by then.

When the ten-year-old Alex arrived to live with Julius and Roxane, after his parents' fatal accident, Julius was already the man whose opinion was sought, who was being invited as an honoured guest, whose phone and mailbox were full of the good opinions of others. Roxane had been his secretary then, as well as his sister. When she left after that terrible row with Julius, he had been quite put out for a while. At least till the new secretary came—a wild, beautiful young man called Sasha who had not lasted very long, despite his passionate admiration of Julius. Or perhaps because of it.

Why had Roxane come back, then? In the years she had been away, there had been very little news from her. A Christmas card, every year, seemingly posted from a different place each time. A birthday card for Alex. And when he married Isabelle, an enormous bouquet of white roses. She had not married, herself, it appeared, despite the child she had borne and brought up. And now the child, the cousin Alex had never met, was grown up, with his own life somewhere in the USA.

Isabelle had said, 'But my God, how chilling!' Isabelle knew where all her family were; she kept in close contact with all of them, and even wrote to distant relatives, exclaiming with real pleasure as she received their letters. Living with Isabelle, he had become uncomfortably aware of such things; his childhood feelings, even those of his young manhood, seemed oddly distant and cold. How could he have accepted such a life? How had he felt, being deprived of his aunt's warmth so soon after the almost unbearable horror of his parents' death? He did not recall feeling terrible distress, as Isabelle suggested he must have. Now he was out of his uncle's world, it hurt to look back on it. Yet it was his own passivity that hurt the most. And the terrible thing was that the passionate man he had become was regressing as the train moved through the countryside; the man who now spent hours on end thinking and talking and loving within his family, and especially with his wife, was turning back into the distant, repressed adolescent he had once been. It was a mistake, Alex thought, coming back, falling in with the old man's wishes like everyone else— the panic of it catching in his throat.

It was very quiet in the train, the noises of people somehow muffled by the stronger sound of the engine swallowing the kilometres. Beside him, a young man turned the pages of his magazine, a magazine Alex recognised as being one Julius wrote for. There was no escaping Julius Newton. He was simply the foremost authority on the links between music and literature, on the rich and strange lives of composers and musicians.

The man next to him wore tiny, neat headphones, and Alex could just make out the murmur of music coming from them. He was glad the man was so quiet and kept to himself. There was nothing he hated more than forced confidences, a stranger's garrulousness. Sometimes, unable to avoid conversation, he had delighted and terrified himself by devising a new name, a new life for himself, as richly textured and exotic as he dared to make it. This was not something he had told Isabelle; she was so at ease with herself that she could not imagine pretending otherwise. The terror won out in the end. Pretending to be someone else might devour who you actually were, he thought, remembering the panic he had felt as a child when somebody, a teacher probably, had called him 'Julius' by mistake.

He must have been staring, for his neighbour took off one headphone and looked at him quizzically. 'Yes?'

He looked younger than Alex, soft-skinned, weak-chinned, slight and very neat, almost polished. Alex flushed. 'Sorry, I was just …'

The man nodded, adjusted his headphones again, smiled politely. He turned back resolutely to his magazine, ignoring his neighbour. But Alex couldn't help seeing Julius' name, and could not force his glance away from what Julius had written. 'Ravel and the Freudians', the article was called, and Alex remembered what he'd heard about Julius' latest project—an 'imaginative biography', as he'd called it, of the French composer, Maurice Ravel. He'd heard something on Radio National about it, not long ago: Julius expounding, in his beautifully modulated voice, on the 'enigma' of the composer.

'And of course,' he had said to the interviewer, 'there'd be no interest if there were no enigma, would there?

That is the task of a biographer, not to explain, oh no, but to probe, to ask questions, maybe to suggest …'

'And it appears that the composer of *Boléro* didn't have a love life?' the interviewer prompted, in a voice of well-bred, steady incredulity.

You could hear Julius smiling as he answered, 'Yes, incredible, isn't it? All the fire, the Dionysian passion in that piece! Do you know, some of his contemporaries in France thought *Boléro* a trifle vulgar—sexy, in fact? Some people have argued it shows an aspect of the composer that does not sit well with the image of his delicate restraint. At this stage in my research, it appears that Maurice Ravel was a man who lived for music.'

'Was he homosexual, perhaps?' the interviewer asked. 'In those days, maybe, one would not have broadcast that fact.'

'One would not have broadcast it to the whole world, certainly,' Julius reproved her gently, 'but Ravel's circle of friends was large and very tolerant. They would have known, if it were true. It's not only this generation which accepts all kinds of sexual behaviour, you know.'

That had been one of his recurrent themes: that each generation thought it was re-inventing the wheel as far as sex or anything else was concerned. Julius had always been good with the sexual side of his subjects' lives, not being prurient or puritanical, but with a nicely balanced delicacy of tone.

His neighbour looked up at him again, and Alex flushed and waved an apologetic hand. He must have been staring at the man, or his magazine. What had come over him? He was not usually rude, even in thought. In fact, Isabelle said he was not rude enough, that he had to learn to be, out of simple self-preservation.

'Please excuse me,' he said. 'I was just interested to see that article. Ravel ...'

'Yes,' the man said, and suddenly smiled.

'I don't understand why people always want to know, to explain, to quantify,' Alex blurted.

'Don't you?' the man said, giving him an odd look. It threw Alex off balance, so that he said, 'No. I don't know why people can't be allowed to keep their own selves private. Why is it that being a creative person seems to allow others entitlement to your soul?'

'But surely that is the nature of creativity, divulging your deepest emotions?' The man's eyebrows were raised, his dark eyes amused. He looked infinitely cool, infinitely in control.

'I don't know,' Alex said. 'Perhaps.' He felt, unaccountably, defeated, even dispirited. He wished the man had a form guide or *Playboy* in his lap; wished that he'd greeted him with cheery, easily defeated masculine freemasonry. There was something about the man's manner that chilled him, that made him want to relapse into silence. But politeness was too much for him, the need to be liked, even by a stranger. He said, 'You live up here?'

The man did not seem to think this an odd change of subject. Still smiling, he said, 'Oh no. This is my first visit to this area.'

There had been no question from him, yet Alex felt bound to say, 'I used to live here. I was brought up in this area, when my uncle moved here in my teens.'

The man nodded, his eyes straying to his magazine. 'So it will not be a discovery for you, as for me.'

There was nothing to say to that. Alex agreed, smiled foolishly, then turned to the window. He had hoped this journey might stimulate in him the need to write again. For a year or more he had been unable to write a single word, apart from his usual facility with preparing lessons. His first novel, so eagerly written and published the year before, had gone almost unobserved. He had written with care and passion; and his publisher's response had been such that he had almost expected rave notices, although he had told himself sternly not to. In the first weeks after his novel's release, he had haunted the bookshops, looking for his book, and although he'd found it in a few, he had been dismayed and then disheartened by the thought of its competition. There were so many books out there, so bright, so colourful, so many with well-known names emblazoned across their covers. What possible chance had his poor little novel, however deeply felt, however well thought out, against that plump cornucopia of words and images?

In many of the bookshops he'd been to, he'd seen Julius' most recent book, a biography of Grieg, in a prominent position near the front desk, and was horrified at himself for the anger he felt at the sight. After all, Julius had bought several copies of the novel, he'd told Alex, 'to give to children of my acquaintance'. Alex had tried not to mind that Julius had offered no comment on the book himself; or that he had suggested in one of his letters that 'writing for children must be a delightful thing to do'. Perhaps he had meant it at face value, as Isabelle had urged him to believe. She had shrugged, rather impatiently, when she saw his reaction. 'Alex, Alex, why do you take any notice, even if this is true? You need to believe in your own worth.'

It was easy for her, Alex thought angrily. She had no need for these things, for her work, illustrating non-fiction books, was its own reward. Or so she always *said*. Sometimes he wondered at her calm, her smiles—was there resentment underneath, boiling away? Thinking about Isabelle in this fashion gave him a cold thrill; she was always so present in his thoughts, his feelings, seemingly even in his body, with such warmth, such insistence, that these stray doubts seemed like a betrayal. *Isabelle*, he thought, and resolved to ring her before he got to Julius' place. At the station, even. He'd say hot, quick words to her, the words she loved, that made her laugh, sharply, with desire.

'So you lived here?' The man's voice startled him. Alex turned back to him.

'Yes,' he said. The other man seemed to be waiting, so he added, 'In the town itself. My uncle wanted the country life, but manageable, you know.'

'And did he like it there?'

'Oh yes. It suited him perfectly. 'And so it had. It was a closed, secretive sort of place, that town, he thought. A place to which Julius never really belonged, despite the fact that he was soon on civil terms with nearly everyone who considered themselves to matter, or that he was occasionally asked to address groups such as Rotary or the Lions. He would do it in his usual light, wry way, sending himself and the others up, but able, somehow, to carry it off without offending anyone. He said it was his 'bit for local culture', the quotation marks firmly, but gently, in place. The move from the big city had made him a mystery, Alex thought. And Julius liked the idea of that. He had done what so many of his colleagues believed to be a foolish, a crazy thing: living life out of the mainstream, out of the main swim of the big cities. But in fact, it had merely added to his aura. Alex had even read a colour magazine supplement article recently about Julius, in which the writer had expounded with awed insistence on Julius' decision to live in the country, as if he were a pioneer.

Now he said to this perfect stranger, 'My uncle was always sure he was right. And he mostly was.'

The man next to him nodded, but said nothing. Was he embarrassed by Alex's sudden revelation, his straying over the border of polite conversation into private resentments? It was hard to tell. People often supposed that conversations with strangers on trains could have this kind of quality, as if stepping into the atmosphere of the train put you out of place and out of time for the duration of the journey. There was something curiously comforting about it, talking like this when you knew you were only to be in each other's lives for a few hours. Alex smiled to himself. 'And now I'm going up to stay with the old devil,' he said almost gleefully. 'For the first time in ten years.'

There was a short silence. My God, it was true. Thirteen years since he'd left Hillview, Julius' house; ten years since he'd stayed for any length of time with Julius. Though of course he had seen him several times over the course of those years. But Alex had not been able to face coming up to Hillview again, till now; and Julius always had so many other claims on his time when he came to the city. He had gone to Alex and Isabelle's wedding, a few years ago, and then to see the twins, when they had just been born. But it was a strange thing that Julius always seemed to manage to upstage any kind of event, so that for quite a while afterwards people who had been guests at the wedding, when they met Alex or Isabelle in the street, would say fondly, 'Oh, and I do hope Julius is well.'

'As familiar as if they'd kept pigs with him,' Isabelle would say, laughing. This piece of French earthiness never failed to amuse Alex. He tried to imagine keeping pigs with Julius, and failed.

He realised that his neighbour was speaking to him, and started. 'Sorry ...'

'It should be an interesting reunion,' the man said firmly, turning back to his neglected reading. Interesting. Yes. As the train swallowed kilometres, and the dusk began to swallow the landscape outside, Alex found that his heart was pounding. His hands felt clammy. He remembered coming home from school and feeling like this; remembered how quiet the house was when Julius was away at one of his festivals and only Mary, the housekeeper and unofficial childminder, was in.

Silence fell on the two men. Around them, people wriggled in their seats, beginning to move belongings from laps to bags, preparing for the stop. A child was swinging on the arms of a seat just up the aisle, and her mother was repeating, 'Stop it, Justine. Justine! I said stop. Justine, please.'

At home, Isabelle would be putting their own Justine and Jean-Daniel to bed, their faces soft and fresh from their bath, the smell of them so sweetly potent. God, how he missed them! They would be wondering why he was not there to tuck them up in bed. In their short lives he had never not been there at bedtime. They wriggled and wanted stories; they would beg for another glass of water, another cuddle ...

Alex had been nearly ten when he had suddenly landed in his father's brother's household, and so had lost that sweet fresh roundness of the young child. Maybe it was for that reason, because the spiky limbs of the pre-pubescent child looked so gawky and angular, that people thought they no longer needed or wanted that intensely sensual love young children receive as a matter of course. Maybe that was what Julius had thought, all those years ago.

two

Alex rode in a taxi through the familiar streets of the town, back towards Hillview. There was a certain something, which he refused to qualify as nervousness, agitating in his chest, and heightening his awareness of everything around him. The driver's large hands lay loosely on the steering wheel, a couple of fingers beating lazy time to a song playing on the radio, a bouncy jazz tune called 'I'm A Certified Senior Citizen'. 'This year it all became clear,' the song went, 'it's a kind of second childhood, do what you want ...' Alex imagined buying it for Julius, smiled to himself at the thought of his reaction. But then, who knew? Perhaps Julius would simply laugh. It was part of his charm, that unpredictability. And he was a fan of jazz, of course. In fact, one of his most popular and impressive essays had been on the art of Louis Armstrong.

The streets were very quiet, as it was Sunday night. The town spread in a long, elegantly elongated U shape up and down two hills and into a valley, and at night this turned into a magnificent stream of black night and the gold and silver light of streetlamps. When he had lived there, Alex loved to go out at night to watch it, that glowing Milky Way of humanity. So many places in Australia, he thought, had an ugly, unloved look, like the suburb he had lived in before his parents' accident, with its straggling lines of drab brick houses, its blue and red and white caryards and hardware shops and takeaway shops—everything with a temporary air to it, as if the whole place was nothing more than a film-set in some complacently realistic movie.

But not this town. Now, the sight of it unexpectedly constricted his heart.

He remembered other Sunday nights, times when he'd hung around the house, hoping to think of something to do. Julius would be working in his study; he would finally call out to Alex, 'Can't you get your paints out or something? Come on, Alex, grow up, be sensible!'

At that time Julius had been determined Alex was good enough to be an artist. He remembered Julius giving him a massive box of paints one birthday, a box Alex himself had dreamt about for some time. Somehow, though, when it was there in his hands, he didn't want it anymore. He didn't want to think about what that meant, now.

'Here we are, mate.' The driver leant over and switched off the meter. 'Not a bad place, Hillview. Heritage place, isn't it?'

Alex smiled. 'Yes, that's right.' Heritage. A word Julius would handle with tongs. But in the half-light of streetlamps, and from the lit-up taxi, the old place certainly looked beautiful. It dated from about 1900 and was of an unusual style Alex had once seen described as Federation Queen Anne: a red brick and light timber exterior, a complex tin roofline, tall chimneys, a small verandah ornamented with carved valances and brackets. The garden of native and exotic plants Julius had planned long ago was now mature. Julius had loved Australian plants long before it was fashionable to do so; he had always loved bushwalking too, Alex remembered suddenly. He remembered being with his uncle in some forest or other, walking steadily along the path, and Julius stopping suddenly, saying, 'Sometimes, I know just why Beethoven needed forests ...' Alex had been fourteen or so, his mind taken up with some private agony, and he had been embarrassed by Julius' unusual exaltation. But now the memory came back to him sharply.

The taxi driver was looking at him strangely, and repeated his request for his money. Alex blushed, and fumbled in his pocket, pulling out his wallet. 'Sorry ...'

God, he was saying sorry to everyone today, acting like a love-struck teenager! It was time to stop, time to do things differently. Time to lay the past.

But when the door opened, there was Roxane. He just stood there for a second, looking at her, hardly believing the change in her and yet wondering at how little she had changed. She had put on weight, mostly around her middle, and her hair was shorter, greyer, too. But she had always been someone who had fully inhabited her body; there was nothing soft or defeated about it, about her, even now. He thought suddenly that she would have been around his age, or not much older, when she'd left Hillview, and was dismayed by the thought. Of course, he had thought her old then, or at least ageless: she was simply an adult, a condition which seemed as remote and unreachable as the moon. But her eyes were exactly the same—eyes of a clear, bright hazel, long-lashed, and the expression in them also as he remembered: direct, but a little shy.

'Roxane!' He dropped his bag and hugged her, smelling the fleshy, rather pleasant scent of her body, feeling the softness of her breasts against him.

'Alex! Oh, it's so good to see you.' She held him away from her, and looked at him with a smile. 'I have to say it. You have grown up. My God, what an inanity!'

He smiled back. 'Well, we all do it.' What did you say to someone you hadn't seen for years? 'It's so good to see you back, Roxane.' But why had she come back? And what had happened to her, over the years? These were questions, he thought, that Isabelle would have put straightaway, quite naturally, but that he could not bring himself to phrase. Privacy, the inviolability of the individual, had been this family's strongest mottoes. How strange to think that Julius, from whom these mottoes came, should have chosen to be a professional eavesdropper, a professional asker of questions.

'Julius is in the living room. We have another visitor,' she said, and picked up his bag. 'Go and freshen up, then join us in there.'

'Thanks, Roxane,' he said. He hesitated. 'There's a lot to catch up on.'

'There is,' she said, direct, unsmiling, but friendly. 'And we'll have time for that.'

He could hear the murmur of voices as he moved down the hall towards the bathroom. Well, if Julius had another visitor it would take the pressure off, anyway. But he was aware of an obscure sense of disappointment.

It was an odd feeling, returning as a guest to the house he had lived in as a child. He knew this house so intimately, remembered small things about it, like the fact that the bathroom mirror had a strange discolouration on one side, and that the hall runner, brought from Julius' city house, Rosedene, had an unusual pattern. The roof—that creaked as it contracted from the heat of the day into the cool of the night—it had kept him awake as a child, some nights, imagining someone walking up there in clumsy steps. Most of all, he remembered this house's smells: they filled his nostrils straightaway, and he understood each of them straightaway, as if he'd never been away. If he closed his eyes, he thought, he would be back there, in the past, standing silently in the bathroom doing what Julius called 'his ablutions', staring at himself in the mirror and wondering who he really was. A kind of panic momentarily filled him. It felt like those dreams when you find yourself back at school, he thought rather grimly. There was nothing dignified about such fear.

No, he was here, in this house he knew so well, as a guest. He would not fall into the house's, into Julius', preconceptions; their relationship was quite other, now—this was not the return of the prodigal son, but a visit from a solid, well-planted adult.

Roxane had put his bag in his old room, of course, and left the door open, so he could go in. He could hear her voice mingling with the others in the living room, and went into the bedroom, shutting the door quietly behind him. He opened his bag on the bed and took out a jumper. Hillview had never been a warm house, except for the living room, which had a large northern window. And the climate in this part of the country was never predictable, especially not in spring. He wriggled into the jumper carefully, the atmosphere of the room folding around him as surely as in the past. When he had finished he stood stock-still in the middle of the room, amazed at the resentment he felt at the fact that the room had been changed. Even the bed was different; it was now a sensibly proportioned double bed, covered with a rich-coloured quilt and plain pale sheets. The bookshelves were here still, crammed with old books. But there was a desk now, and a well-upholstered chair, instead of the old table and wooden chair Alex had used. There were new pictures on the walls—of course, Julius would not have kept the *Lord of the Rings* calendar or the photos of glassy surf and quotations outlined in red that Alex had tacked up. The room opened on to the verandah, but there were new curtains over the French doors, and even the carpet had been changed. It looked like a room in a pleasant 'atmospheric' guesthouse, and Alex bit his lip to try and stop the images of the past from welling up in him, but couldn't quite suppress them.

This room had been his kingdom, and nobody disturbed it, certainly not Julius, and not even Mary, the woman who kept house for them after Roxane had left. Alex was a tidy child, and so he had been allowed to do his own housework. Here, Alex had spent much of his time, reading, writing, dreaming, and studying French, his favourite subject at school, much to Julius' delight—and sometimes playing loud rock music. Once or twice Julius had knocked on his door, asking in that light, firm tone of his if Alex would mind turning that music down. He was always very careful to say 'music' and never 'row' or 'noise'. Just once he had observed that the trouble with rock music was that it was trapped in simplistic frames. Alex had not argued, had not known how to. He had simply stared, silently, and wished his uncle would leave him alone.

Now he left the room quickly, and walked towards the living room. No-one would be surprised that he had taken so long to front up. Julius had often said that a person needed to gather their strength for meetings with others. Particularly with family. He would understand, he told the teenage Alex, if he wanted to opt out altogether and, at the time, it had seemed like a relief. Now, though, he was a parent himself, and he was not sure anymore.

He went into the living room, and was immediately dismayed. There, sitting in one of the tall brocaded chairs, was the man who had been sitting next to him on the train. He must have come here straight after arriving at the station, while Alex had been ringing Isabelle. But what was he doing here? And, oh God, what had Alex said to him on the train? He remembered only too well.

'Ah, Alex!' In that moment of dismay, Alex had failed to register Julius' presence, but now he saw his uncle properly, as he came forward to greet him. He got another shock, for Julius had aged, quite noticeably. His hair was quite white, his frame looked frail, his hands felt dry. But their clasp was still strong, his eyes behind wire-rimmed glasses still intelligent and amused. Alex felt an unexpected surge of affection for him, and said sincerely, 'Julius, it's so good to see you again.'

'Likewise,' his uncle said, and walked back to his chair. That was about as much as you could ever hope to get from Julius. The old bewilderments, the old confusions, surged in Alex for a moment, and then receded. His uncle could not help being how he was, who he was. Alex looked at his aunt, sitting opposite him, calmly sipping at a drink, and she looked back, her eyes betraying little.

'I understand you and Mr Pym have met already,' Julius said.

'Charles, please. Or Charles Joseph, if you prefer. I do use both names,' the man said, smiling thinly. Obviously he had decided to play it cool. Alex looked at him. He was really a singular-looking personage in many ways, with his gently waving, gleamingly brushed head of ash-brown hair, soft, pale cheeks as smooth as a child's, and clothes as perfect and well-pressed and curiously old-fashioned as if they had been made of stone. He looked like he belonged on an ornament table, or in a park—he was a creature as candied in his own confection as some kitsch Victorian *tableau vivant*. Isabelle would enjoy him, Alex thought; her pencil would fly over the paper, mimicking the way he folded his arms, the way his ankles crossed so tidily.

'Well, Alex, Mr ... er, Charles is staying with us for a while. He is helping me with the Ravel biography. In fact, doing much more than helping me. Charles has brought some extraordinary things to show me, things which will turn the whole established view of Ravel upside down!' There was a strange quality to Julius' voice, a strained excitement that troubled Alex.

Charles Pym smiled thinly, but said nothing. Alex, feeling he had no alternative, murmured, 'So that is going well, Julius? I heard a couple of things ... it sounds very interesting.'

'Yes, yes,' Julius said rather impatiently. 'I have already done a great deal of work. But what Charles has brought throws another light onto the whole project.'

Alex waited for the portentous revelation, but Julius did not explain. Pym steepled his fingers. His glance towards Julius was kindly; even, Alex thought, a touch proprietary. He was surprised to find that this shocked him a little. How well did Julius know this man?

In his teenage days, he had occasionally wondered just what Julius did, had done, for sex, or love, or whatever you wanted to call it. Women had come to the house, but there had never been any kind of suggestion that any of them had been more than friends. Men also. Julius seemed to be either utterly, incredibly discreet, or else without any sexual interests at all. Now, watching Pym's indulgent glance, Alex wondered. Poor Julius, he thought, if it is that, fancy falling in love with a creature so palely perfect! A creature who looks like he wouldn't understand passion if it hit him on the head.

'Mr Pym ... er, Charles has been helping me with suggestions over the last few months,' Julius said, sounding a little, and rather unusually, flustered. 'He has been most generous with his time, sending me things, talking to me on the phone. Now it is a very great pleasure to meet him at last.'

Alex looked across at the other man. He looked back politely, but without any interest. 'You are too kind, Dr Newton,' he said.

'It all sounds very nice,' said Alex, rather sharply. Roxane looked over at him, and smiled. Her glance at her brother and Pym was neutral, yet once again Alex was aware of something else in the air, something he couldn't quite put his finger on.

'It took Julius till well into dinner before he remembered about you and the children,' he told Isabelle that night. He'd needed to speak to her again. 'And then he asked after you only perfunctorily. Everything is centred on Ravel and that blasted Pym guy. Nothing changes. You know, it was funny, now I remember exactly how it was, how he had these massive enthusiasms while he was writing a book, sometimes just for his subject or someone in that person's life, or for someone he'd been in contact with over that time.'

'That's kind of touching, isn't it?' Isabelle said. 'To be centred to that extent.'

'I'm not sure that it isn't just simple selfishness,' Alex said. 'No more. Once he's got Ravel out of his system, he'll also drop this Pym.' Maybe this is it; my poor old uncle at his age is vulnerable to all kinds of inappropriateness. And who's to say I wouldn't be, at his age, with time on my tail, he thought, without saying anything. Aren't I condemning Pym rather rashly? What do I know of him? Surely I'm old enough now not to judge. ... or is it *du dépit*, as Isabelle would put it: because I had sweated on this reunion more than I cared to admit?

'But what is it that Pym has brought him?' Isabelle's calm voice penetrated his thoughts, not commenting on her husband's view of Julius. 'Has Julius said?'

'Oh, Julius loves mysteries. Who knows? It's something only Ravel freaks are going to care about, I suppose. This Pym fellow is apparently a musician himself. Julius says he's quite well known, though I can't say I've heard of him ...'

Isabelle laughed. Alex could picture her, in her shabby dressing-gown, flung on after her bath to answer the telephone. The cord was frayed, the soft cotton would be brushing the roundness of her body.

'You're jealous of Pym,' she said. 'Alex, admit it. You wanted to have a proper reunion with your uncle, and he's stopped you.'

The picture of her grew in his mind, and he imagined reaching under her dressing-gown, cupping her breasts, smelling the nape of her neck. He said softly, slurringly, What are you doing right now, Isa? Tell me ...'

'Standing here,' she said, 'talking to you. What do you think?' But there was a teasing note to her voice, because she knew what he meant, exactly what he meant, and wanted to spin the pleasure out further.

When he finished the call, he went back into the kitchen to get himself a glass of water. Roxane was there, alone, drinking some fragrant herbal tea, her hands tight around the cup. He sat down next to her.

'Everything's fine then, at home?' The expression of detached interest in her eyes was one he remembered well. She had asked him all the requisite questions at dinner, and Julius had even put in a few of his own. Yet it was obvious that their minds, and particularly Julius', were on other things. And Pym, ever so quietly and discreetly, always brought the conversation back to Julius himself. He had rabbited on for a full minute, at least, about some interview he was supposedly aching to hear, a radio interview with Julius about his time in France during the war. Julius had smiled courteously, self-deprecatingly; but when Alex chimed in with a mention of Isabelle's father, his eyes looked distracted again. Alex felt bereft. He had come a long way, he thought, as he looked at Roxane. A long way for all this. But he knew the rules.

'Everything's fine, yes. But what about Julius, Roxane? What about this Pym guy? What's going on?'

'I don't think the years have improved my perceptions of Julius.' Roxane smiled. 'And he's the same as ever—guards his secrets closely.'

'But did he know this man before?' He hesitated; was not sure whether Roxane would understand the peculiar feeling Pym gave him, decided not to mention it.

Roxane looked at him, then shook her head. 'There have always been people around Julius, admirers,' she said slowly. 'But this fellow ... I don't know ... he doesn't strike me as ...' She shrugged, as if deciding something, and he cursed himself for not having the courage to challenge her. 'He seems to be genuine enough. But Julius ...'

'Yes?'

'He's fragile ... There's something, I'm not sure what, some kind of hunger in him. Long-distance correspondence can lead to some odd situations, you know. And Julius has been needy for years.'

Alex stared at her. 'Surely not! For as long as I've known him, he's been self-sufficient. I've never heard him express a need for any other human being.'

'He'd never say it. None of us learnt to say it, except for your father, Alex. That was part of the whole thing of growing up in our family.'

'But surely not ... Pym.'

She looked at him ironically. 'It happens, you know. And even more so at Julius' age, if that's what you're thinking. It's odd, Alex, there's something about that young man that reminds me of Julius himself. But that's simply unfair of me, trying to say Julius can only love his reflection. Julius is a total amateur in these things, you know, Alex.'

Alex smiled with disbelief. 'But all those things he's written about, he understands ... Remember the Beethoven book, those extraordinary passages on love?' He'd loved that book; how acutely it spoke to his adolescent self, to his yearning to be consumed by passion.

'Writing and doing are two different things ... Many writers say that, you must know that yourself, Alex. You can open your mind and your senses to a world of things through writing, things you could never do in real life. Julius has always been afraid, afraid of passion. But then—' She broke off abruptly.

He waited, feeling the moment grip him by the throat, knowing now that things could never be different in this family, that all would remain unsaid. And then she sighed. 'But then, maybe, we are punished by our own failings. None of us is immune from that, even my poor brother.'

He was chilled by the weary pity in her voice. It had been a mistake to come here, he thought. When he said goodnight, too quickly, he did not ignore Roxane's wry expression, but was glad to put it behind him.

three

In his dream, he is lying spoon fashion with Isabelle in their bed, his arms around her waist, her head under his chin, her buttocks curving against his groin, and he is deep inside the deepest flowering softness of her, groaning, murmuring. Gently, they are rocking together, slowly, tenderly, as if the night will never end, and the incoherences of love are all that are real. Then he is awake, with a throbbing kind of groan that shakes the sleep from him all at once, the bed wet beside him, the grief of not finding Isabelle there beside him shattering him. He stumbles out of bed, suddenly desperately needing to pee, and remembers to pull on a T-shirt and pants before heading clumsily into the hall. He could walk this place blindfold, finding the dark bathroom as much by instinct as by logic. The bathroom window looks out on a night full of stars, and for some reason this strikes him as an amazing thing, so beautiful that he stands there staring. Coldly they burn, he thinks, silent and terrible and lovely almost beyond bearing, and the words of Rilke, words he'd written up and tacked on his wall as a teenager, come back to him:

> *For Beauty is nothing*
> *But beginning of Terror we're still just able to bear*
> *And why we adore it so is because*
> *Serenely it disdains to destroy us ...*

Along the hall, there is a light still burning under Julius' door, but in the rooms where Pym and Roxane presumably lie sleeping, there is nothing but darkness. He remembers that Julius has always worked till late in the night, never getting up till eight or so in the morning. When Alex returns to his room, he sees the telephone lying coiled up on the desk, and nearly calls Isabelle again, to tell her of their dreamed lovemaking. But he stops himself, instead sitting down at the desk, and pulling his notebook towards himself, begins to write.

> Sometimes Julius forgot that I was not part of his usual audience, and he would tell me stories about his time in France, during and after the war. It was those years that had changed everything for Julius. His father had always talked about how his eldest son, the only child from his first marriage, was too soft. Those years shut him up, Julius said. He had loved the army. Its careful discipline, its passionless purpose pleased him; and he had enjoyed the circumscribed friendship

that it afforded him. Because he spoke very good French—an asset insisted upon by his mother—he had been seconded to the British forces fairly early on; not for him the jungles of South-East Asia or New Guinea. Yes, the army had been good to Julius, but he had left it without regret. It had never been in his plan to stay with it, and never in his nature to indulge in regret. And of course that had been when he first discovered France. France at the end of a bitter war, a war that had been as much civil as external, a war of brother against brother, a war whose scars had still not healed. Julius came to a France exhausted, broken, both deeply suspicious and utterly relieved. It was a dangerous time, when the country could have plunged headlong into military dictatorship or total anarchy. He witnessed the summary execution of militiamen; watched the pain and hatred welling into faces—a hatred, he said later, as much directed against the liberating forces as against the German occupiers and the Vichy servants. It was a hatred of his own good fortune as a representative of a nation that had had no such moral abyss open before it; hatred of blind fate that had dictated that some be born to this, others to that.

He writes till his hand aches. Then he stops and looks at it, and smiles. How extraordinary. After a year of not writing, this is it. And what it looks very much like is the beginning of a life. The biography of the biographer. The thought is pleasing. A deep calm settles over him as he returns to bed. In seconds he is asleep, dreamlessly now.

In the morning he was up early, feeling fresh and cool, despite his disturbed night. It was still very quiet in the house, and Alex tiptoed around, as much for the house's sake as for its human inhabitants. As a child he had always imagined that houses had lives of their own, which they began as soon as their humans were asleep, or away, and once or twice, he'd tried to catch his house at it, pretending to be asleep, then opening his eyes suddenly. It seemed to him now that the house creaked with dismay around him; a dismay born of the fact that conventions were not being observed. Alright, he told it silently, alright, you can get on with it, I'm going outside!

Out the back was Julius' vegetable garden, truly his own, unlike the garden out the front, which was maintained by a weekly gardener. Julius had always loved this place: he said gardening, especially vegetable gardening, was a wonderful hobby for a writer, for it forced you to think carefully, to stop and slow down and plan. Alex had loved it too, but had never wanted to do any of the work. It was cooking that appealed to him, the fast, explosive mix of ingredients, the magical transformations and transmutations that resulted. He rarely followed recipes and sometimes had bad results; but somehow, it never worried him. Mostly, it worked. Mostly, it satisfied. Gardening was too slow, too painstaking, too Julius, he thought, amused by himself.

At this time of the year the garden was full of new green things. Already bees were looting the flowers of various plants: tall thin clumps of rocket, black-and-white butterfly-blooms of broad beans, a few early strawberries. There were spring onions and artichokes and peas as well, all at a young, tender stage, not yet producing food; and the structures left over from last year's crops of beans, of hops, of snow peas and corn. There was something rounded and gentle and exciting about this promised bounty, this miniature fertility. Julius had made sunken sawdust paths, and raised beds, rich with dark soil and clumps of horse and chicken manure, and in one corner were his bins, holding compost at various stages of decay. Down past the bed that traditionally held potatoes he had planted swards of clover and vetch that now spread their lurid green over the ground.

Alex thought of days when he had flung himself down on similar patches of clover and watched the sky, arm held up against his eyes to shield them from the sun. He did that now, even though the clover was a little cool from the night, and the sky still rather pale. But the sun prickled at the edge of his vision, sparking multicoloured filaments of light along his arm, his jumper sleeve, making his lashes tangle with the tinselly sparkle. The sun was not yet very hot, but still it seemed to trickle into every pore of his skin, every nerve ending, till he felt as full and light as a balloon. Would modern children, his children too, brought up on sensible precautions about the sun, miss out on this? Too much was sensible these days, he thought, too much was explained, quantified, no time left for meaningless gestures, useless rebellions, incoherence and unanswerable questions. Too much riding roughshod over the little sparks of the senses, too much living in the mind.

And so it had been with him too, for a long time. It was seldom that he simply sat or lay, like this, singular and yet enveloped in the world around him. He sat up, rubbing his back, watching his shadow, idly wondering at the way it was a confirmation of solidity. Imagine you see someone and they have no shadow, one of his mates at school had said once. What would happen? What would you do? It seemed extraordinary that such a small thing could cause any problem, yet everyone had said they would be afraid, horribly afraid. The lack of something so insubstantial indicated a lack of presence, an absence of substance itself. It was the same with a reflection.

The garden gate creaked. Alex turned his head and saw Roxane coming towards him, already dressed, carrying a small basket. She smiled at him. 'You're up early.'

'So are you.'

'I thought we might have asparagus with melted butter for breakfast, with an omelette. I am so tired of muesli and yoghurt!'

All at once, Alex was aware of just how empty his stomach was. 'What a fantastic idea! Why do we always feel we have to keep to a few breakfast things only, while we'd be furious if we had to eat the same thing dinner after dinner?'

Roxane crouched by the asparagus plants, deftly cutting the fat spears that poked out from the ground. 'Habit, I suppose. We are all creatures of habit.'

'Even you?' he hazarded. 'After all the different places you have lived, the different things you've done?'

She sat back on her heels and looked at him. 'Of course. Especially me. Moving can be a habit just as much as standing still, you know.'

'Were you happy, Roxane?' he said, without knowing that was what he had been going to say.

She considered this seriously. 'Yes, at least some of the time. When I wasn't happy anymore, I would move.'

'Is that why you came here?' He could feel his palms prickling with the danger of these questions. Being a family didn't entitle you to know everything, Julius had always said. It did not give you ownership rights, exclusive licence to other people's souls. But Roxane did not flinch. She had been long away from Julius. Or perhaps it had never been her way. After all, what did he really know about her?

'I came here,' she said, 'because Julius needed me.' She got up, wiped her slightly dusty hands on her trousers, and picked up the basket, now quite full of plump asparagus. She looked at Alex, and smiled. 'It is no answer, is it, Alex? And yet it's true. My son is grown up now, he has gone away and believes he does not need me anymore. And I was more alone than I could have thought possible. So, when Julius' letter came, it seemed the right thing to do, to come back.'

'But Julius isn't sick, is he?' Perhaps that was the clue to his frailty and to the otherwise inexplicable need for family close by him.

'He isn't sick, at least not like that. Oh, he does have some bone thinning, a man as skinny and delicate as Julius is always going to have trouble with that. But there is something else, Alex—a fragility that I had never seen before. A brittleness. I'm sure you remember that he never used to talk about his books till they were finished. With this one, though, he can't help himself. It is too close to him, too close to his real self, I think. And so he talks and gives interviews and scribbles copious notes but doesn't get down to the real business. That is why that man Pym is here, I think. He wrote to your uncle a long time ago, a fan letter after he'd read the Beethoven book.'

'But ... is that all there is to it? I thought at first, well, they're like disciple and master, embarrassing perhaps, but ...' He wanted to say more, but wasn't sure how to phrase the vague unease he felt.

'Well ...' She gave a little smile, shrugged. 'I'm not sure, Alex. Not at all. But ... I'm here, now.' They looked at each other, eyes full of remembered moments when Julius had seemed so in control, so much a master, and they merely trailing in his wake.

four

Julius and Pym did not come out of the study until quite late that evening. Julius was looking very pleased. He even made a joke or two, which Pym laughed at discreetly.

'Charles has just reminded me that it's time for that interview.' A small laugh. 'Of course, I do like to keep an ear on how they edit these things. I have been burnt by journalists before!'

'You can't be too careful, Dr Newton. That is very true.' Pym was sipping his brandy, watching as the radio was tuned, the positions assumed for listening. He caught Alex's eye, then looked away. The theme music for the interview segment warbled on, seemingly endlessly, and then, suddenly, there it was, Julius' voice, a perfect voice for radio, clear and low. Alex looked at his uncle, sitting upright in his chair. There was no false modesty there, no great interest either. Just a courteous listening, as if it were someone else whose voice was being carried on the airwaves.

'I sometimes think we in Australia are on permanent holiday,' Julius said. 'A holiday outside the course of history. We do not always understand the way fate both shapes human beings and is shaped by them. We believe that every person is responsible for their own life; we have never been blown away by the whirlwind of time. That's what I saw in France. I saw people like myself who had been put, who had put themselves, into situations which I could only imagine. It was not a question of "there but for the grace of God"; it was an understanding, for the first time, that between us, between people, there could be immeasurable gulfs, abysses of terrifying depth. Sometimes, I was mistaken for an American, and the looks in people's eyes as they said that!'

'Were they angry? Jealous?' the interviewer asked.

'There was jealousy, yes. But also resentment, a subterranean thing, a wish to punish as well as to atone. They knew the Americans had saved them from the Nazis. But they also knew they had been saved from themselves. Yet they did not feel understood, deep down in the abyss, by the Americans. They felt the Americans had no conception of the abyss. And so their feelings were complicated.'

'Was it different when they knew you were Australian?' the interviewer asked.

'Mostly people did make the difference, and they had a much softer view of Australia. I came into contact with many ex-Resistance people too, and they had the same feelings—suspicion of the US as well as gratitude, and a gentleness towards Australia. Partly that was through ignorance, you understand—very few people knew anything much about Australia, and many wondered even why we were in the war, as we were seen as almost falling off the map of the known world. But it was also because Australia was seen, I think, by Europeans, as a country of perpetual sunshine and brave men, different from Britain and the US in all kinds of ways. The British were seen as Europeans like the others: wily, old, patient, tenacious. The US was seen as a world power, but an immature one—loud, rich, generous, clumsy. And Australia—well, Australia was a nation small enough to be cherished, large enough to be worth commenting on, if not exactly large enough to be factored into world power struggles. Mind you, most people had very odd ideas about us; but the fact remains that they were mostly favourably disposed. I remember one time at the beach in Biarritz, in '45, yes, it must have been then. I had gone there on leave, you see, after VJ Day. All the coast of France had been occupied by the Nazis from the beginning, of course. There were still bunkers on many beaches, on cliffs, that sort of thing, and mines. You had to be careful. Biarritz's image as a resort for the wealthy had taken a pounding of course; like the rest of France at the time it had a rather down-at-heel air to it. But it was still beautiful. Still very much the place Maurice Ravel had loved so much, before the war. Yes, I was interested in Ravel then, I had a kind of fellow feeling for him. I had gone to see his house in Saint Jean de Luz, though I did not know at the time I would be writing a book about him and—'

'Of course, Ravel was Basque, wasn't he?' the interviewer chipped in eagerly.

'Yes, he was Basque. On his mother's side. And Swiss too, of course, on his father's side.'

'What a combination! Basque fire, Swiss precision.'

'Indeed. So there I was, on the beach, looking out to sea. There is something marvellously repellent about the sea, isn't there? That ceaseless, relentless flow, the sand, smooth as paint, sheened over and over by tireless waves … I was looking at it, and thinking of what it represents, for us human beings: death perhaps, or more frightening still, vast, impersonal, relentless life, or, more simply, timelessness. It was odd, in a way, this vast thing, so blindly purposeful, out there, in front of my eyes, while at my back was the cauldron of our history. Neither to be fully understood; neither to be denied. It was then that I knew, that my vague longings for my life after the war crystallised. I knew I would be a writer. And that I would write about music, the one art, it seems to me, that unites both time and timelessness.'

'Yes …' the interviewer's voice was almost a whisper.

'There was a small family walking along the beach, coming towards me. There was a woman, two children. They had obviously seen me from a distance, and they smiled shyly as they came closer. I wasn't in uniform, but I suppose my clothes, my haircut made it obvious that I was not subject to the same rationing as they were. One of the children, a little boy, whispered, *"Monsieur ... l'Américain,"* and I was suddenly taken by the look in those eyes; the dignity, in spite of the awe. I said, *"Non, je suis Australien, moi,"* and I dug in my pockets and found some sweets, which I gravely handed to them. I watched their faces breaking into delighted smiles, just as much by my speaking French as by the sweets, I think. The little boy hopped up and down on the spot, like a kangaroo, and his sister smiled politely. The woman then begged me to excuse the children's high spirits, and told me that the "poor little things" had lost their father during the war, and that their mother had been ill for years. We shook our heads over the sadness of it and watched the children playing, and eventually walked on in different directions. I have never forgotten that little moment; to me, it represented so much of what had happened, and so much of what was in store—the sadness, the hope, the crushed lives, the possibilities.'

As the interviewer thanked Julius, and the theme music of the programme swelled under his farewelling voice, in the living room the four of them sat in singular silence. Then Julius sighed, and got up to switch off the radio.

'Well, they didn't do too badly. They did cut some, but you've got to expect that.'

'It was a great interview, Julius. Very moving. 'Alex could hear his voice quavering a little.

'Thank you, Alex. You never say all you want to, but ...'

'You said just enough.' Roxane suddenly reached over and patted her brother's knee. He looked astounded, as well he might, Alex thought with an inward smile, but he soon recovered.

'Most impressive. Extraordinary,' came Pym's cool voice. There was an unreadable expression in his flat pebble eyes. But all at once, the moment had shifted and changed. Julius got up, said that really, he was very tired now and might turn in. Alex began collecting glasses and cups, Roxane helping him. Only Pym remained in his chair, finishing the last of his brandy.

Days later, Alex still could not understand why Pym ruffled him so. After all, the man was a pleasant enough companion, often smiling, well-read, clever enough to be quiet when it was the right thing to be, and to make good conversation when it was likewise necessary. It was simply a feeling, of the kind you couldn't really explain or even talk about—an unedifying emotion which worried him more by what it revealed about himself than about the surely harmless Pym. Not everyone, after all, could be vivid and tactile; there were some, like Pym, who seemed almost like messengers from another world. And yet a completely modern angel of the Annunciation, Alex thought, curiously an artefact of the modern world despite his anachronistic clothes and manner.

Pym turned out to be a good, even excellent, pianist, and in the evenings played a few pieces, always gracefully, never sentimentally. Alex watched him as his thin fingers moved over the keys, watched his quiet face not changing, and marvelled inside himself at the antipathy such a person could produce in him. He made light of these emotions to Isabelle, but found himself startled by the intensity of them. And Pym, though treating him always with scrupulous courtesy, seemed nevertheless to sense his feelings, and to be amused by them. Yet Julius seemed quite unaware of any 'atmosphere'. He always had been good at ignoring it, always.

The first couple of days had passed slowly, tentative conversations established, tentative roles defined. Julius had spent much of them in his study, first alone, then closeted with Pym, and emerged at lunchtimes with bright spots in his cheeks, his eyes shining with a febrile gaiety. Alex had seen a variation of this gaiety before, when his uncle had been in the middle of a book that was going particularly well, but never as strong, as excited, as unnerving as this.

On the second afternoon he had walked down to town with Alex, but without Pym and Roxane, who had both pleaded tiredness. On the way uncle and nephew had spoken lightly, affectionately, about the past; it was simply not possible for Alex to speak in any other way, nor for Julius to listen. And then Julius had finally spoken a little about what Pym had brought him, incredible papers, he said, which showed that the supposedly solitary and self-sufficient Ravel had fallen desperately in love towards the end of his life. More: that under love's influence, and just before he had been stricken with the terrible brain disease that had eventually claimed his life, he had written a quite extraordinary piece of music. He said that Pym had brought the papers, and that so far they looked genuine. His voice was trembling as he spoke of these things, for they affected him deeply, much more deeply than anything Alex could have said about their shared past. But strangely, he did not resent this, understanding Julius' excitement, feeling closer to him than at any time since he had arrived, although he found his obsession with the French composer tiresome and even rather tedious. For the first time in his life, he knew that he loved Julius. He had never understood that before, for love had always been something other than this strangely circumscribed, elusive thing. And even now he could not be sure that it wasn't Julius' advancing age that had induced this awareness. Julius was old, and the feeling of fear which that brought in its train was mingled with the inarticulate affection. If only they had learnt to speak, long ago!

And that evening Pym had played for the first time, something which was to happen regularly during Alex's visit. Alex had planned to stay a week with his uncle and aunt. But he wondered if he should shorten his stay, wondered if after Julius' birthday he could take himself off. He was slipping into old habits here, those of silence and the swallowed word, of subtle glances and withheld gestures. In that atmosphere even thoughts of his wife and children, dearly held to him, sometimes seemed to break loose from their moorings, so he would ring Isabelle up in a kind of panic.

'I miss you terribly,' he told her. 'And the children ...' He could hear them burbling in the background, not yet old enough to say anything intelligible to him when Isabelle put them on the phone, and quickly tiring of the strangeness of hearing his voice without seeing him. 'I miss you all.'

'We miss you too,' she said, but sometimes, in his treacherous heart, he wondered. Without her, he felt almost like a ghost, without a shadow, without any real definition. But she would always be as he found her: solid, real, vivid. She would miss him, yes, but not in the way he missed her. He said as much to her, and she laughed.

'Alex, Alex, you think too much of me.'

'Why, don't you think of me, Isabelle?'

'Of course I do. But I do not wonder all the time what you are thinking of me. That is because you are a writer, I think. Writers think too much. They look at themselves too much. Other people, we do not examine ourselves in this way.'

'But don't artists think like that, too? You look at the world, you give it form on the page too, you need to know what you are looking at.'

'Oh yes. But that is different. We do not need to know what is inside us or inside others when we paint. Even when that comes out on the page, or the canvas. It can be understood not only with the mind but with the body. And it does not need to be understood at all.'

'I don't believe that, Isabelle. That notion of the artist as unconscious. You are not like that at all. You are not naive. And you do understand other people.'

She laughed again. 'Yes, perhaps I am being too extreme. But then you can drive me to that, my love. Now, Alex, what is the latest on Mr Pym?'

She was a connoisseur of Pym stories now, and Alex took delight in collecting them for her like beads on a thread. How Pym, almost incredibly, had taken out a snuffbox one evening, a silver, intricately carved flat box in which lay not snuff but thin strips of paper-wrapped chewing gum. He had gravely taken one, and handed the box around. How Pym had told Roxane that his grandfather had once been asked to play on the *Titanic*'s maiden voyage, but had refused on account of his bad feeling about it. How Pym had played his way through one Ravel piece after another, gently, while Julius sat and listened. One afternoon, Alex had come in from the garden, for a storm was approaching. He had gone into the living room to find Pym seated at the piano, immobile, listening to one of Julius' many recordings of *Boléro*. At that moment, the sky had darkened, and a great gust of rain had come in from the west, sweeping up clouds of steam before it. Somehow it had sent a shiver down his spine, the silent man sitting there so still, intently listening, the music building up relentlessly, almost blindly, and the storm outside.

'Did you ever read what Vincent d'Indy, who was a contemporary of Ravel, said about Ravel's music?' Isabelle said when he told her.

'I have read barely anything about Maurice Ravel,' Alex replied. 'He's not one of my favourites, you know that, Isa.'

'Well, we learnt about him at school, you know. He's supposed to be one of the true manifestations of eternal Frenchness. Anyway, d'Indy said that Ravel's music was always portentous, but that it was an empty portentousness, it was striving after effect. Perhaps that's what your Pym is doing.'

'Perhaps he's a reincarnation of Ravel,' Alex said frivolously. 'That's why Julius loves him so. Because Ravel represents everything he loves best, everything he can safely love without being bloodily involved.'

'Poor Julius,' Isabelle said. 'Do you know, Alex, I think I would be afraid of you, if I didn't love you.'

Sometimes, he told her, silently, after he'd put the receiver down, I'm afraid of myself too. I don't know whether I can trust myself, whether I will always know who I am, who I am supposed to be at any given time.

He watched his uncle and Pym in the evenings after they emerged from the study where they spent most of each day. He watched for signs of fluster, of brighter eyes, but always, there was nothing. Nothing but a certain tone in Julius' voice, which Alex refused to characterise as a plea. Nothing but a certain satisfaction in Pym's movements; not a sensual satisfaction, but something more elusive, more remote. It was like nothing Alex had ever seen before; and yet there was a nagging familiarity to it.

Pym's eyes gleamed dully behind their glasses. His voice was light, curiously unaccented, almost sexless. His hands moved often, giving the impression of alacrity. His skin bloomed softly, giving an illusion of sweetness that was immediately dispelled by those eyes. Alex had always thought only pale eyes could be so ... stony, unreflective. But the brown gaze of Pym was flat, hard, unreadable.

And Julius? Well, he was the same as ever, the same, and yet with that new frailty, that new excitement, that sense of being suspended over something momentous.

five

Alex walked with Roxane in the golden light of late afternoon. They were going to do the shopping for Julius' birthday party, which was to be held the next day.

In this season the trees were magnificent, displaying tender new leaves. Alex thought of the last commission Isabelle had done, her favourite so far: a book on trees. For months she had worked on it; for months the whole family had heard, seen, nothing but trees. The work had taken them to all kinds of places, all kinds of moments, moments now forever associated with the trees they had seen: a short scabby orange tree growing wild beside a railway track, laden unaccountably with the juiciest fruit; a long olive line of forest on a flat horizon; a huge old pine creaking above an abandoned house; a palm, shock-headed as an ostrich, craning its trunk against an extraordinary, turreted yellow house; a magnificent white box gum with a cubbyhouse poised precariously in its branches; thin, shabby coastal scrub; delicately foliaged casuarinas with their sturdy trunks. Isabelle had taught him to look at the tops of eucalypt trees where the tender new leaves—pink and yellow—grew; had made him catch his breath at the strange, almost frightening sight of the green rash of life creeping over fire-blackened trees; and especially had shown him the light. How it fell on these different trees, native and exotic, in such different ways: on European trees, the leaves merged into a brilliant translucent blur of colour, while the Australian trees' leaves glittered singly, each a point of light. In one suburb they saw them both together: a gigantic gum and a massive elm, each firmly rooted, each beautiful, but so different in their reception of this brilliant, hard light. It was no wonder, Isabelle said, that the first European painters here hadn't actually seen what was in front of their eyes: it would have been like being on another planet. As it had been for him, when he'd gone to France, after school.

Paris had been a shock, an astonishment. Its legendary elegance had hidden other things, which Julius had not dwelt on—pounding torrents of cars and the frightful sound of traffic; the windows of North African cake shops in the Latin Quarter, full of toppling green and pink confections; the sordid fear in Pigalle; the haggard faces of beggars, their aggressive, obsequious warnings—*Monsieur, j'ai faim!* In that Paris, he saw the Paris of Villon, of Quasimodo, something he had not expected from Julius' descriptions. And when he travelled south, moving frequently, he saw more and more Frances, each more different than the last. Once, he had stood transfixed in the steep streets of the ancient Gascon capital, Auch, his ears full of a medley of church bells, carried perfectly to him through the still, glassy sky. It had riveted him, that moment; it had seemed to define something so perfect, yet so out of reach, something for which he would always reach. A few days later he had gone to Toulouse, where he met Isabelle ...

In the street across from them, a man was video taping, walking backwards, his eyes intent on his lens, getting everything into the camera as it happened, as if his whole life were a film. Alex saw Roxane watching him too, and smiled.

'I wonder if you know what it all means if you've got it on film?'

'Perhaps,' she said. 'But then, you do that too, don't you Alex? As a writer?'

He nodded. 'I suppose it's the same impulse.'

'But in writing you can edit better,' Roxane said.

'That's true. All those hours stored on video. And all it does is remind you how inconsequential real life is. Makes you think it's a bit of a fraud, writing—imposing order, playing God.'

'But there is a shape to things,' Roxane said. 'In the end. I've seen that many times over the last few years. Maybe writers are just better at spotting line, order, in what seems shapeless to the rest of us.'

It was easy then to ask her. 'I never have known what you did, Roxane, for all those years.'

'Oh, I was a teacher.' She smiled. 'A teacher of sorts. I qualified, you know, years and years ago, before I left Julius.'

He was struck by her choice of words, but said nothing about it. 'I can understand why you came back, now! Sometimes I think teaching is the enemy of any kind of normality.'

She looked at him smilingly, raising her eyebrows. 'Oh no, it's another attempt at shaping. I loved it, Alex. But I found … well, that I maybe did not have much to offer anymore. My life became too barren.'

And that's why you came back here, to Julius, he wondered. 'But your son …'

'Seth has made his own way,' she said. 'He does not need me at the moment.'

'But that's maybe not true,' Alex said. 'Often at that age you need your parents more, even as you push them away.' He was surprised by his own vehemence.

'He doesn't,' she said, very definitely. 'His scheme in life does not include a dull, careful mother. And that is fine.'

'I will never do that with my children!' Alex cried, before knowing he'd stepped over some kind of boundary. What the hell. There were too many boundaries in this family, too much abdication.

Roxane looked at him a little sadly. 'You will not have the choice,' she said. 'Later.'

'Oh, I will,' Alex said fiercely. 'I will make it happen. You have to. It, life, them, us, it's all too precious … We just can't …' He could not finish his sentence, the words were too hot and bitter for his throat to release.

'Alex ...' Roxane touched his arm. Their eyes met.

For months after his parents' deaths he had lain awake imagining that if only he had gone with them on that fateful journey, it wouldn't have happened. They would probably have left earlier, and so they would not have arrived at that intersection at the same time as the runaway truck. Or perhaps they would all have caught the train, for Alex loved trains, and his parents would have wanted to please him. He'd forced his eyes shut, replaying that moment in his head, the moment when he could have said, 'Mum, Dad, I don't want to go to school today, can I come with you?' and then things would have been utterly different. But he'd had no premonition, just a bit of crossness that they had gone off for the day while he was stuck in the hot classroom doing a maths test. It was there that the principal had come for him, her kindly face quite white with shock. Alex's best friend, Miller Cameron, had nudged him as he went to go out. 'Hey, what're you in trouble for?' And he had grinned back. Oh, God ...

'Sometimes you have to make things happen,' Alex said again, too loudly, gulping with the effort. 'You have to force life, force the reactions of others.'

Roxane said nothing. They walked in silence for a while, then she said gently, 'Alex, you have not told me much about your life, your work, your family ...'

So he told her, and she listened, even while they wheeled the trolley around the supermarket.

That evening, Alex lay on the bed in his room, unable to settle to anything. Roxane was working in the kitchen but had declined all offers of help, and Pym and Julius were closeted together in the study once again. Alex had rung Isabelle and she had said that everything was fine at home, that he was not to worry, that he should stay a few days more with Julius and Roxane. She would maybe come up then, for it was about time she met Roxane, and besides, she and the children needed a breath of country air, she had said, and Alex could hear her smiling.

It was terrible, he thought restlessly, how a place could have such an effect on your nerves, on the very self you thought you had figured out. Lying on this bed, in this room, it was as if all the years in between had not happened at all. Even talking to Isabelle on the phone had not grounded him firmly in his own reality. This contrasted with the feeling of the room: despite its change in furnishings, despite his own feeling at first that the room had changed, it had not, fundamentally speaking. It was as if all the inertia, the torpor of his teenage years, was here with him, right in this room. When he looked back to those years, he was filled with a kind of horror: not for anything would he have gone back there. And yet, he thought, I write for that age group; what does that mean? He had grown accustomed to thinking of that time with a kind of repulsion—but had the seeming paralysis remained within him, merely waiting for a chance to creep out again? The dreamy, aimless, pessimistic boy who had lain on this spot, if not in this very bed—was he still there, really? Was his presence more real than that of the loving, determined, optimistic man who had taken his place? Or were each creations, inventions, obnoxious to each other but yet not quite, not utterly true?

He swung his legs impatiently off the bed, got up, walked to the bookshelf. He squatted down and looked at the books. Among the old paperbacks were a few books he remembered from childhood, and he thought perhaps he might ask Julius if he could take them home. He pulled out one after the other, remembering precise occasions he had read them, with a painful clarity. *The 13 Clocks*—oh yes, he had been puzzled by James Thurber's humour, not quite sure if it was funny or not; KM Peyton's *Flambards*—oh, how romantic that had been!; and the Moomintroll books, nearly all of them, neatly standing in a row, their much-handled covers speaking silently of long hours of reading. The early books had been vivid, bright, sparky little pictures of family life, but later they had become much more gloomy, introspective, culminating in *Moominpappa at Sea*. He had read that one twice, fascinated despite himself by Tove Jansson's relentless Scandinavian whimsy, her delicate picture of the sea, of boredom, of alienation, of loneliness, willing himself into that odd state of suspended animation that was the mainspring of the story. He opened the book at random and began to read.

> The crystal ball was always cool. Its blue was deeper and clearer than the blue of the sea itself, and it changed the colour of the whole world so that it became cool and remote and strange. At the centre of this glass world he saw himself, his own big nose, and around him he saw

the reflection of a transformed, dreamlike landscape. The blue ground was deep, deep down inside, and there where he couldn't reach Moominpappa began to search for his family ...

Alex remembered the Groke, too, a strange, cold creature that loved light and needed it, despite the fact that she killed everything around her in her lonely love. For her, time was without end, punctuated by the occasional lamp.

Time passed slowly in a book like that, in a state like this. Time had no meaning, it seemed. Everything would always be like this.

Alex slammed the book shut and put it back on the shelf. He moved resolutely to the French doors and stepped out onto the verandah.

SIX

The timber floor was warm under his feet in the late sunshine, and he stretched and looked out into the garden. Beyond the garden fence were neighbouring houses, and Alex could hear sounds coming from them, the squeals of children, the squeaks of washing-lines being loaded. Two tiny birds with pale yellow breasts hopped unconcernedly on the grass near the verandah, while an evil-eyed magpie swirled enchanting water music in its throat.

'Beautiful, isn't it?' Alex turned to see Charles Pym standing there.

'Certainly is.'

'I prefer a music box to a nightingale,' Pym said, and then he laughed. 'Baudelaire. Always ready to shock, and even bore.' He added idly, 'I was named after Baudelaire, you know.'

It was the first personal remark Alex had heard the other man make. 'Always thought Baudelaire was rather overrated. All that stuff about the loneliness of the artist, the albatross who can't walk,' Alex said rudely. As a matter of fact, he had first come across Baudelaire's poetry in French, at school, and had deeply loved it. He had spent days reading *Les Fleurs du Mal*, the words stirring in his heart and his head, and the poem that had most moved him had been 'L'Albatros'. He could still recite the words in his head, the French words that he had never been able to adequately translate, but whose meaning had struck him then with the force of truth. '*Ses ailes de géant l'empêchent de marcher* ...' 'His giant's wings prevent him from walking,' just did not have the same lonely dignity.

Pym's flat eyes regarded him steadily. But he made no direct response. Instead he said, 'Being faithful to an attitude can be difficult.'

'It's a bit late in the day for this, isn't it?' Alex said, hating the words even as he said them. Why did Pym bring out the prig, the boor, the philistine in him? If it had been him and Isabelle discussing Baudelaire, or even Roxane or Julius, it would have been quite different.

'You are right,' Pym said.

Come on, crank up another subject, Alex thought, see how good you are at making even an idiot like me feel at ease.

'You said it was your first time back for years,' Pym said carefully. 'Are things still as you knew them?'

'I suppose so,' Alex said. 'Things don't change, do they. Only we do.'

'Oh, but I disagree. Things exist in the eye of the beholder only.' His stony eyes watched Alex carefully, a little smile playing around his mouth.

Alex looked back defiantly. He spoke rapidly, harshly. 'And you have known my uncle for a while?'

Pym made an airy gesture that forgave Alex for the rude suspicion of his tone. 'Why, yes. Dr Newton and I have corresponded for some time. We met briefly in the city, and I told him about the new evidence I had discovered, and so he invited me here.'

'Why didn't you write your own book, based on this new material?' Alex couldn't believe it was himself—sweet-natured, gentle, or at least diffident Alex—speaking.

But Pym merely smiled faintly. 'Oh, I am not a writer. I am a musician. I do not have Dr Newton's facility with words, I am afraid. And he is a well-known figure, of course, both here and overseas. Who would listen to an unknown such as myself?'

'But why not take it to France, where surely there are more Ravel specialists?' Alex heard himself arguing.

'I did not want a specialist,' Pym said. 'I wanted someone with the warmth and brilliance to make a leap of imagination, to understand truly what he had come across. A versatile gardener like Dr Newton can be much more successful at that than a botanist of musical growth, listing taxonomies endlessly.' He smiled. 'And besides, Dr Newton is one of a rare breed—Australian, but European too, understanding of intricacies but no respecter of hidebound procedure.'

Alex's head was filled with Pym's bewildering yet apt metaphors. 'Well, and so what do these papers reveal?'

'That is not in my province,' Pym said firmly. 'I am merely the bringer of news, not the analyst.' He smiled faintly. 'The annunciator, not the writer of gospel.'

A chill gripped Alex. 'Where did you get them?'

This time Pym's expression showed some reproach, whether at the abruptness of the question or the suspicion behind it. He said a little stiffly, 'I have come to an agreement with Dr Newton that this will not be revealed to the public at large until we are sure of the authenticity of the papers in question. However, I can say that they came to me through unusual channels.'

'I see,' Alex said lamely. If this had been a duel, Pym had well and truly won. The forgiving smile he bestowed on Alex showed this, even if nothing else had done.

'And you are a writer yourself, Mr Newton, I believe?'

'Alex, please.' Even as he said the words, he wished he could take them back, remembering those fairytales where giving your true name meant handing over your soul, your power. How ridiculous. Pym was no mythical being, no creature of dream or nightmare. He was real, indisputably there, flesh and blood and prone to all the strange embarrassments of the human condition. Alex added, quickly, 'Yes, I write children's books. My first novel came out this year.'

'Ah,' Pym said. He looked out at the garden. 'A difficult thing to achieve, I believe. Many of us forget our childhood, is that not so? It is a rare thing indeed not to do so. Maybe even abnormal.'

'Perhaps.' Alex did not want to be included in this man's assessments. Strangely enough, though, he could easily imagine Pym as a child. A miniature version, he'd have been, one of those children who never change, who are like small adults. He'd have had those stony eyes behind thicker glasses, his limbs smaller, his skin softer. But that's all. One of those children who would stand and watch you; whom even the bullies, the hard cases, wouldn't go near, because of some indefinable aura. Not like Alex himself had been, at least after the accident: shy, repressed, and quiet because of it. But no, Pym would have been, instead, watchful. And fearfully knowing.

Alex made an effort. 'My uncle says you are a well-known musician. You work mostly in Sydney?'

'Dr Newton is too kind. I am merely a session musician. I have worked all over the world.' He did not seem interested in saying any more about himself. There was not even in him the irritating, but comforting, familiarity of the egotist. Alex remembered Sasha, the secretary Julius had once had. He had been handsome, conceited, but openly adoring of Julius. Had Julius and he ...? But no, Julius had never given any signs of anything. But maybe it was as Roxane had said—he was afraid of passion. And so he would have pushed Sasha away, driven him away with his fear, yet been unable to still his yearning. No wonder he had given him the sack.

'I find your line of work interesting indeed,' Pym said, regarding Alex thoughtfully. 'I was reading a biography not long ago of Lewis Carroll, and it was most extraordinary. A happy childhood, he'd had. And it was with children he was happiest, as an adult. Not unlike Ravel, in many ways. Ah, Dr Newton!'

'Well, a fine day, is it not?' Julius was there, smiling, looking fresh and rested after his nap, and plainly not suffering. Alex watched Pym as the latter smiled back and said something innocuous. I am simply imagining it all, the strangeness, the mystery of the man, he thought. That has always been my refuge from Julius: secret imaginings, attempts at theories out of Julius' grasp.

'This is quite like old times,' Julius said. 'Isn't it, Alex? You, me, Roxane.' Pym smiled discreetly. 'Those were not always easy times, Charles. We were not used to children, Roxane and I.' He touched Alex lightly on the arm. 'Not easy for you, I know.'

Alex did not know what to say. Julius' words fizzed in his mind, stung; yet they did not feel intimate, because they were spoken to Pym as much as to him. He wished he didn't always have to notice such things, wished he could have responded to Julius in the natural way Isabelle would; but he could not. He simply murmured, through a tight throat, 'These things are never easy, are they?' and could have wept at the relieved gaze Julius turned on him.

Julius had always talked a lot about being an adult. He told people how he did not remember his own childhood much at all; how he had always been conscious of being not so much young as immature. The short memoir he had written on his childhood had been much praised, with its gentle raillery, its charming wit, that of a full-grown man looking back over his earlier powerlessness—none of the joy or terror, the hot, overwhelming emotions of childhood. And he'd always treated Alex scrupulously, asking his opinion on small things, though not major ones. The French tradition had it right, he was fond of saying. A child was an *adult en herbe*; he needed to learn quietly, by example, not by being encouraged to be a *chien savant*. The current Anglo-Saxon way of making childhood into a space of its own, an enchanted otherness, led to many problems, he said. To the separation of child and adult, so that the child was no longer father to the man, but eternal child, who could not father anyone, least of all himself.

Least of all himself ... Alex watched Julius chatting happily to Pym, the latter responding with that careful gravity, which was actually, he realised with a shock, a kind of fatherly indulgence.

seven

Morning, another day. Roxane was in the kitchen, sitting at the table, sipping a cup of coffee. She smiled a little wanly at Alex when he came in. 'Fortifying myself for the task ahead.'

'The task? Oh, Julius' party.' Alex poured himself a cup and sat down opposite her. 'It's going to be some do, isn't it?'

'I don't know what's come over him. He never used to take much notice of such things.'

'It's that man Pym.' Alex could not keep the spite out of his voice.

Roxane looked at him steadily. 'Oh, I don't think so.'

'Well, good morning everyone.' Here was Julius now, up early for a change, freshly shaved, his skin glistening palely. He was smiling, and rubbing his hands like a villain in a melodrama. 'What a lovely morning!'

And so it was, with an overarching sky billowing silkily, glazed with fresh light. The day before had been bright enough; but here was its apogee, a morning as fresh as a painting.

'Happy birthday Julius,' Alex said, giving him the present he had hastily chosen in the city, just before leaving. Julius unwrapped the package and took out the CD it contained. 'Oh, Alex. How kind of you. I've been promising myself this treat for so long! Thank you so much. I am so glad you were able to come and stay with us.' He laid a hand on Alex's shoulder. It trembled a little—it spoke of his age, his frailty despite his fighting mind—and Alex was more moved than he cared to admit. He tried to fill his mind with thoughts; thoughts of himself old too. Odd how the body changed so much, but not the spirit, at least to oneself. And at such a time in history, when people were expected to stay young for so long, ageing was especially a burden.

'I'm glad you like it, Julius.'

For answer, Julius slipped the CD into the player kept on the kitchen dresser. The strangely uncertain then stately sadness of Liszt's *Vexilla Regis Prodeunt* filled the room, and Alex bit his lip, looking at Julius and remembering what he had read about the composer's state of mind when he had written it. Lonely, isolated, unable to find meaning in much anymore, he had turned to God and produced this unexpected piece, which veered from beauty to sadness to an underlying terror, and finishing in such a disconcertingly pretty way. He watched Julius' face but could read nothing there, although he was obviously listening very carefully as the music moved into the well-known strains of 'Sursum Corda'. Not for the first time he wondered what music actually meant to Julius. He knew so much—he understood and loved it, yes, as a gardener, not a botanist of music, humbly and with great delicacy. But did the shards of it enter his spirit, wound him, transport him? Who could know?

All his childhood, even before his parents' deaths, Alex had been listening to music; it had filled every room he lived in. Even in a lift he could not ignore the piped music, and it bewildered him that so many people would not even notice its presence. He felt it, with every straining nerve, just as, sometimes, snatches of unheard music would fill him utterly. Music, it seemed to him, was the true essence of reality, the one art most able to bridge the gap between the senses and the mind. Yet he had never tried to study music himself, had never imagined that he could ever play or indeed had ever wanted to.

'Julius,' he said, before the moment ended. 'Isabelle and the children, they would like to come up and see you and Roxane too. Would it—'

'Of course. You hardly need to ask, Alex,' interrupted Julius, waving a hand. 'Of course they must come. I will be looking forward to seeing the newest members of the family again. They change so much at that age, don't they?' He smiled, and it seemed to Alex, for a moment, as if there was indeed a common bond joining them all, a circle that could expand, fill in.

Roxane said, 'But they must come up as soon as possible! I haven't even met any of your family, Alex!'

'He's a dark horse, our Alex,' Julius said, smiling. 'Always was, isn't that right, Roxane?'

Roxane smiled discreetly. Alex stammered, 'Thank you, Julius, Roxane. I know they will all very much look forward to …'

'How nice to hear Franz in the morning,' Pym's voice said from the doorway.

Even Julius looked a little nonplussed, but he soon recovered. 'Alex's present,' he said, beaming.

'Ah yes, Alfred Brendel playing, if I'm not wrong?'

Of course you're not wrong. How can someone like you ever be surprised, Alex thought resentfully.

Pym sat down at the table and buttered a slice of bread. 'I'm afraid, Dr Newton, that I did not think to bring you a birthday gift.'

'Not a problem,' Julius said, rather awkwardly. 'Why should you?'

'I think that gifts from strangers can be a burden rather than a blessing.' Pym poured a cup of coffee. 'They put giver and receiver in a false position.'

'Quite, quite.' Julius got up quickly and turned the music down. 'I do not like to make a fuss of my birthday. Never have.'

'Until this year,' said Roxane, rather sardonically.

'That is only to please my friends.' Julius smiled shyly.

'I like grand occasions,' Pym said, seemingly unconcerned that he was contradicting himself. 'We need ceremony in our lives, we post-religious people.'

'Oh yes, oh yes,' Julius said. 'More and more, I feel that. We do need to have a sense of ritual.' His glance at Pym said, Well done, thou good and faithful servant. Yet Pym smiled his indulgent smile.

'Charles and I will have a surprise for you, too.' Julius addressed a bemused Roxane and Alex.

Pym bridled. 'Oh, Dr Newton, we must keep it a secret till then! And remember, we have all those people in the city to see …'

Julius flushed like a naughty child. 'Of course, Charles, of course. 'Alex wondered rather sadly, Who is the parent in this relationship, who the child? He had once read of a famous writer who, at Julius' age, had fallen madly in love with a man much younger than himself, whom he had characterised as 'my son'. Was this what was happening here? The human heart knows no bounds, he thought, no limits. He had no idea what drove someone like Charles Pym, and was not sure he wanted to know. A shiver rippled down his back as he caught Pym's eye. But there was no blank, pitiless Greek god looking out from there, no recording angel. They were the pebble eyes of a shallow, showy modern man whose every gesture, every thought, seemed planned and controlled and analysed.

'That reminds me, Alex,' Julius said, still rather awkwardly. 'Charles and I are going to the city tomorrow. We'll be away for quite a little while. However, feel free to stay, and have your family up here. I'll be glad to see them when we get back.'

Alex saw the rapid, quickly lowered glance Roxane threw at her brother. He began, 'I will …'

'Of course, Roxane told me you had long-service leave, so I know time won't be a problem for you.

Fancy you having long service leave, Alex! It's something I've never experienced.'

'Nor I,' said Pym, his gaze humorous. Alex felt his neck grow hot.

Watching Julius among his guests, Alex thought he understood why he had moved to this place. Here were no big egos all struggling for possession of the field; there was room for only one or two, with lesser ones worshipping at the shrine. Julius walked easily among them all, looking every centimetre the dapper national treasure he undoubtedly was. He introduced Alex to a few people, and Pym to a few more, and talked about people Alex had never heard of. His manner was expansive, cordial, *épanoui*, as Isabelle would have said. He was full of something, a lightness, a brightness that seemed new.

Roxane handed around trays of drinks, of food that the caterer had delivered that afternoon. She raised an eyebrow at Alex, and then moved around in her turn, accepting curiosity and indifference equally calmly.

I can't stand parties, Alex thought. You can't talk properly, or even hold anyone's gaze for long. He felt like a block of wood around which tides swirled. What was wrong with him at the moment, that he couldn't take part in even the smallest, simplest human interaction without being paralysed by its lack of meaning? Everyone knew the rules of this kind of thing; some people actually got sustenance from it. So what was so different, so special about him that he couldn't even pretend? Why should he be so arrogant as to think that everything must be real? Why couldn't he simply play, tinker, reinvent like everyone else? People would look at him, their eyes slide past, because that difficulty lay like a cloud over him, a reproach to them.

Roxane handed him a drink. 'You look bored, Alex.'

'No, not bored. Just …'

'I know. It astonishes me, how much of a chameleon Julius is.' Her eyes, watching her brother, were rueful. 'It used to impress me so.'

'It still does me,' Alex said honestly.

'You and thousands of others.' They watched Julius talking with the mayor, his thin pale face listening carefully to what the woman was saying, his eyes attentive yet gently ironic.

'She'll go home tonight and think she's met a kindred spirit, and never forget it,' Roxane said.

'And he'll have forgotten it in an hour,' Alex continued. They looked at each other, and smiled.

'What cynics we are,' Roxane said lightly. 'Come to the kitchen with me, Alex, help me load up more food.'

The benches and table and dresser were covered with food, perfect this afternoon, still fresh and gleaming tonight. Alex filled a tray with bowls of olives decorated with tiny slivers of sun-dried tomatoes, heart-shaped smoked salmon sandwiches, artichoke hearts on pale crispbread.

'Elegant food, hmm?' Roxane said.

'The kind you need to eat for three hours before you can fill up,' Alex replied. Roxane popped an olive in her mouth. 'There is something worrying you, Alex, isn't there?'

'And you,' he retorted.

'Oh, it's nothing, for my part. Just a kind of resignation. When I left, Julius was just the same. I can't really justify to myself why I came back.'

'Nor me. Beside Julius, Roxane, I felt, I feel, so ... incomplete, so ... hollow. Sometimes I think I have gone way beyond him, but it's not true.'

'Oh, but you have. It's Julius who hasn't. He stands still. It took me some time to see that.'

'And then there's Pym. It worries me, Julius' friendship with that man, and I don't know why. Julius was always so careful with his friends, his intimates.'

'My dear boy, don't worry. If there is something predictable about Julius, it is that he is careful. You can be sure he knows just who Pym is, and has been checking up on him. But he's a secretive man. Pym is his discovery. And he is canny, too. He wants to keep Pym's discovery of those papers to himself.' She balanced the tray carefully and walked to the door. 'We may as well enjoy ourselves, Alex. Or at least be resigned.'

But Alex stayed in the kitchen for a while longer, looking at everything around him as if seeing it all for the first time. Through the half-closed door, he could hear the first notes of something or other Pym was playing. It was not something he knew—something harsh and silvery all at once, a trickle of notes that burst into a jazzy torrent. And the music filled his body, the torment of it, the terror, the pity. It grew under Pym's long thin fingers, grew like something that had no business there, in that room full of eager chatter. He saw Julius standing, by himself for once, for a moment, watching Pym play, listening. And there was an extraordinary stillness about him, just for that moment, a leashed excitement that made him wonder whether he had ever really understood his uncle at all, ever.

And then the clapping, the congratulations, Julius stepping forward, face flushed, one hand up for silence, honouring Pym, who nodded his head in a gesture that should have been humble but that seemed, somehow, triumphant. Their eyes met; and Alex saw an expression in his uncle's eyes as they rested on the pianist, an expression he never forgot, unreflected in the dark eyes that faced him. And in that moment, he started to feel slipping away from him the old images, the old emptiness. He would do it, he thought. He would write a life of his uncle, he would lay the ghosts for all of them. The new understanding inside him, the tenderness it gave him, that meant it would be right. But still, it felt like a loss, this new knowledge, as well as a liberation.

Part 2

BEFORE

Extracts from
working manuscript of

The Pursuit of Beauty:
A Life of Maurice Ravel

by Julius Newton

(to be published by
Symphony Press)

NOTES FOR CHAPTER ONE: 'The Enigma of Ravel'

When one allows oneself spontaneity, one babbles and that's all. In art, everything must be thought out. Massenet, who was so gifted, squandered his talents in an excess of sincerity. He truly wrote everything that came into his head, the result being that he always repeated the same thing: what he thought were innovations were nothing but reminiscences. The truth is, one can never have enough control. Moreover, since we cannot express ourselves without exploiting and thus transferring our emotion, isn't it better at least to be fully aware and acknowledge that art is the supreme imposture? What is sometimes called my insensitivity is simply a scruple not to write just anything.

Falsehood taken as the power of illusion is the only superiority of man over the animals; and when it can claim to be art, it is the only superiority of the artist.

(Ravel, *La Petite Gironde*, July 12, 1931—this passage queried as to authenticity ... His brother Edouard said it was a forgery. What did MR say? Silence on that matter.)

He was open to passion, 'I am Basque, the Basque feel deeply but do not show it.' He suspected the motives and emotions of Beethoven and Berlioz—too contemplative, too mystical: in that lay danger. His idol is Mozart 'in the contemplation of beauty', not truth, or passion.

See here for what Poe said: 'Passion can only degrade, not elevate the soul.' M. R. no Poe or Baudelaire, for all that he admired them, however. Not tormented in the showy way that they were; he was a man of elusive discreetness, of exquisite sensibility in music that was matched by his personal life.

POE'S INFLUENCE ON RAVEL (SOME NOTES FOR CHAPTER THREE: 'The Albatross and the Abyss')

Does Poe appeal to the French because of his dense intellectuality; there is no real emotion, it's all in the head, even when he's preoccupied with horror ...

Poe himself, in 'The Philosophy of Composition':

Beauty is the sole legitimate province of the poem. A few words, however, in elucidation of my real meaning, which some of my friends have evinced a decision to misrepresent. That pleasure which is at once the most pure, the most elevating and the most intense, is, I believe, found in the contemplation of the beautiful.

> When indeed men speak of Beauty, they mean precisely, not a quality, as is supposed, but an effect—they refer, in short, just to that intense and pure elevation of soul—not of intellect, or of heart—upon which I have commented, and which is experienced in consequence of contemplating the 'beautiful' … Now the object, Truth, or the satisfaction of the intellect, and the object, Passion, or the excitement of the heart, are, although attainable, to a certain extent, in poetry, far more readily attainable in prose. Truth, in fact, demands a precision, and Passion, a homeliness (the truly passionate will comprehend me) which are absolutely antagonistic to that Beauty which I maintain is the excitement, or pleasurable elevation, of the soul.

(Ravel thought of music thus; his copy of this article is underlined.) Also:

> The fact is, originality (unless in minds of very unusual force) is by no means a matter, as some suppose, of impulse or intuition. In general, to be found, it must be elborately sought, and although a positive merit of the highest class, demands in its attainment less of invention than negation.

'A supreme imposture'—Ravel refers to this article as a 'hoax' on Poe's part—he was a genius of invention, a teller of exceedingly tall tales. And certainly original! And is this how we understand a hoax, an imposture? Isn't there sterility at the heart of imposture? Whereas in Poe's work, there is a beating, bleeding heart, a torment. Poe's stories are often cruel—but cruelty is often the other side of pain.

But for Ravel, no cruelty. Rather, an intellectual approach nevertheless exquisitely calibrating emotion? A delight in the artefact yet a broad tenderness—much more encompassing than Poe's.

See also: Baudelaire:

'I love a music box better than a nightingale'—and yet: '... music gives the impression of space, it hollows out the sky; it transports me like the sea ...'; 'music above all else ...'

'The great artist consults nature for the elements of his work, as a writer may consult a dictionary for the elements of his; neither nature nor the dictionary may be equated with the finished composition.'

'Dandyism is a form of male artificial beauty vastly preferable over nature.'

Imagination and control

'Peasants love sculpture but are unmoved by the finest painting. I dislike sculpture because it is closest to nature.'

Realism is anithetical to Baudelaire's nature, and thus he talks of a painting: 'Where one should be looking with a painter's eye, the public seeks only truth.' So you have this farce of people looking for things in a painting as if it were from real life—is this so for music too?

Strangeness, ornate surroundings, oriental luxury: Ravel might have had those influences, but his life was ordered and tidy, not at all like Baudelaire's.

NOTES FOR CHAPTER FIVE: 'An Intelligent Art'

Important qualities in MR's art: sensuousness, humour, elegance, reserve: a terseness of logic, particularly attracted to originality in idiom and texture—it 'must have something to say'—purity and omnipresence of melody characterise Ravel's work—Debussy's is more elliptical.

As a child MR was sensitive to every kind of music (see here 'the roots of emotional response to music planted during first few years of life').

Ravel the perfect, consummate composer—liked to draw attention to his art as well as spinning webs of magic in his music.

MR constantly strove to remodel himself—loved diversity, ceaselessly exploring varied domains—he was a master of irony and deadpan humour with a reserve of feeling even stronger than Debussy ... tact, discretion', totally against the romanticism of the Germans: sought a purer, lighter art, an intelligence utterly musical in all its sensitivities.

The secret of Ravel's music (from the Revue Musicale *devoted to Maurice Ravel, December 1938)*

If I close my eyes and I evoke the pleasures born in me to the sound of Ravel, it seems to me that the most astonishing, the most vivid were those pleasures for the ears, for the nerves, in fact, purely physical pleasures, but also, amazingly, intellectual, indirect joys in that sense.

Joys reflected back to one through intelligence. The overt or covert denial of intelligence has for too long weighed heavily on generations of artists—and yet not a dry one, not a frozen or dull one, but an intelligence of the world, of the senses, an intelligence that was not only in his art, but in his person. He had some constant, sure friends. And he never forsook or deceived them. But he also practised, with extreme delicacy, that sacred egoism of the artist which serves to preserve the spirit and talent against all parasites and toadies.

Secret is a word often associated with Ravel—and a secret, real or supposed, is often the best line of defence against the importunate flies that buzz around success.

So what was Ravel's secret? Perhaps simply a respect of his work, of the job he was here in the world to do, his taste for proper techniques, in a neat, properly arranged setting, the artisanal sense of well-made work, and of material perfection, and that passion, so French in its essence, for the beauties of grammar and the graces of syntax!

cf. Tristan Klingsor:
> *And the ironic and tender heart beating under*
> *The velvet waistcoat of Maurice Ravel.*

NOTES FOR CHAPTER SEVEN: 'Never Alone, Always Solitary: Ravel the Man and his Friends'

Why did he never talk of any attachments? Did he have none, or was he simply discreet almost to the

point of sickness? Or was he a man not of words—
'everything is in my music'.

He hated racism of any sort—many Jewish refugees from the early years of the Hitlerian regime came to see him at his house in Montfort l'Amaury (some of whom, of course, were Marta Susskind and her family). He had also, in the First World War, refused to take part in the jingoistic condemnation of German music which some musicians had tried to force on everyone; and because he had actually fought in the war, his attitude, though decried, was grudgingly allowed to stand.

He had many friends—he had a gift for friendship. And he loved children. Even in grand company he would immediately gravitate to children, play games with them, on their level. He loved unusual things, cunning little contraptions, things of beauty and delicacy and weirdness.

He was a great gardener, growing all kinds of plants, but especially the shapely, the beautifully textured or coloured or else the amazingly huge or ugly, 'all kinds of mottled plant monstrosities'. An intense love of beautiful fabrics, shapes, etc, but not opulent—a kind of sumptuous simplicity.

Proud to be Basque—referred to it often. Referred to his ancestry and birth there with love and tenderness and also a certain wistfulness:

> Moreover, there is the light; it's not like the relentless sun found in other parts of the Midi. Here, it is delicately brilliant. The people feel it: they are agile, elegant, and

their joy is not vulgar. Their dances are nimble, with a restrained voluptuousness. Religion itself, though devoutly observed, is mixed with a grain of scepticism.'
(letter to a friend.)

Yet he was Swiss, too, from his father, and intensely French. Did he become so loved by the French because of his contradictions, not in spite of them—for they made of him a glowing whole?

Is his life, his art, not such a pursuit of beauty but a reflection of it?

NOTES FOR CHAPTER TWENTY: 'The Last Years' (Ravel's illness—adapted from an article appearing in *Brain* in 1948)

Ravel's brain illness was indeed a curious one, for it affected written and spoken language, especially the written, without in any way affecting his thoughts or appreciation of music. The dreadful thing was that his capacity for composition remained unchanged in his head; but it was almost impossible for him to put those musical thoughts onto paper. Or even to play them on the piano or any other instrument. The illness caused a veritable dissociation between musical thought and musical expression. The patient recognised all notes and was able with great delicacy to point out false ones; but was quite unable to pick out all notes correctly on the piano himself. Although he was able, for a while, to still write down notes, he made many errors, and was eventually unable to do this at all. For four years the patient was trapped in a hell which can only be imagined.

cf. Hélène Jourdan-Morhange's testimony as to her friend (from **Ravel et nous,** *1945):*
Ravel could not write his name anymore: my son Philip wanted, on this particular morning, for him to sign a photograph, and he had to ask another friend to help him, he was desperate ... Alas! When people asked him, after the last concerts, to sign ... he would move away from them like an automaton, looking like a haughty man even though his heart was nigh to bursting with bitter sorrow. At the beginning of his illness, Ravel fought, reared against it, telling us off for not telling him exactly the words he was looking for, then his pain became more secret. He only wanted to be alone, in the end. I remember seeing him at his house in Montfort l'Amaury, seated in an armchair ... his gaze lost in the distance. I said to him, 'What are you doing, dear Ravel?' and he answered me simply, 'I am waiting.'

Why did Ravel's death, expected as it was, touch so many people? Perhaps because he was the last Proustian representative of an age that in those desperate, dark times of the late thirties, when the world was fast unravelling, might have been seen both as a golden age and a lost opportunity. Yet Ravel, despite his Symbolist dandyism, was no anachronism. He was fully aware of what was happening in the world, and he understood the terror and horror that was to be unleashed on the world, and perhaps was glad to be going from it. Yet his terrible illness did not distance him from people; the bitterness of it did not curdle him completely. He inspired universal affection and respect, even amongst people who did not love his music.

the documents

10 Rue du Helder, Biarritz,
Pyrénées Atlantiques
France
August 7

Dear Dr Newton,

Some years ago, I wrote to you expressing my appreciation of your wonderful and highly unusual book on Beethoven. Since then, I have read anything of yours I can find; you are indeed a fluent writer and a great judge of character. I understand you are now planning a biography of Maurice Ravel. It may interest you to know that I have certain papers in my possession which may be useful to you in this task.

Sincerely yours,
Charles Joseph Pym

★

FAX TO DR JULIUS NEWTON
FROM CHARLES JOSEPH PYM
Biarritz, August 20

Dear Dr Newton,
                Although I cannot divulge to you all of what I have, suffice it to say that it would be of the utmost importance in any Ravel biography, for it proves beyond doubt that the composer did indeed fall in love, and had an important relationship with a young woman towards the end of his life. I know that you are very keen to peruse the documents, but I would like the opportunity to bring them directly to you when I come back to Australia in three weeks time, as I explained on the phone.

Most sincerely,
Charles Joseph Pym

★

FAX FROM CHARLES PYM
TO DR NEWTON
Biarritz, August 22

Dear Dr Newton,
                I am much looking forward to meeting you and giving you the papers. I am very grateful for your offer of credit in your book, and offer my services as your scribe and general help. I am enclosing a photocopy of the work which I referred to in our latest telephone conversation.

Yours sincerely,
Charles Joseph Pym

★

January 25

To Geoffrey Zauber
Editor, *The Lyre*

Dear Geoff,
        Here's the article we collaborated on for the special Ravel issue. You will notice it is in the style of French magazines of the thirties. Also an evaluation of the sonata. Let me know if you need or want to make any changes. *Arts Today* is also running pieces, but the enclosed, as we discussed, are exclusive to you. Look forward to seeing you on Tuesday.

All the best,
Julius

NOTES FOR AN ARTICLE ON *LE GOUFFRE*, *(THE ABYSS)*, by Maurice Ravel (1934), for autumn issue of *The Lyre*

This piano sonata appears to be Ravel's last work, undiscovered till the present. It is a brilliant piece of innovation, moving in its conception, clever in its phrasing, with a structure both coherent and daringly experimental. Jazz motifs abound in this work (NB Ravel's fascination with, and admiration for, the jazz mode of his time). But there are also other influences at work here—something of the hectic brilliance of *Boléro*, the sprightliness of *L'Enfant et les sortilèges*, the magic of *Daphnis et Chloé*, the sombreness of the 'Kaddisch'. There are also echoes of Basque musical motifs, an indication that this piece was probably composed at

Ravel's beloved Saint-Jean-de-Luz. If I'm not mistaken, also, a hint of the kinds of tones found in Javanese music (we must remember that Javanese and Balinese music had found an astonished audience in Ravel's generation). Also, a rising tide of passion and despair not found till now in Ravel's work characterises this unusual piece (cp notes on Ravel's illness). Indeed, it could be said that the sonata almost encapsulates Ravel's life and influences.

The sonata is very distinctly in three parts, and notes in the margin of the work indicate the movements even had distinct names: 'Avant', 'Devant', 'Le Gouffre'— 'Once', 'Before' (or 'In Front Of'), and 'The Abyss'. These appear to correspond with distinct emotional states (cf notes on Ravel's love affair with Marta Susskind). We can speculate as to the nature of these, but the music itself appears to suggest that the composer's equanimity was severely shaken by these experiences, and that his despair at a lack of a happy resolution was complicated by the despair of his terrible illness. After 'The Abyss', there is silence, an abrupt, total, terrible silence, both in the music and in the composer's ability to create (cf letters to his friends, notes). The title of the work itself appears to refer to the notions of Baudelaire and Poe as to the fear of the abyss, or the void.

The importance of this work? Immeasurable. Once and for all, it lays to rest the fallacy that Ravel was a composer of brilliant idea but emotion so delicate as to be absent. Here is a brilliant demonstration of his genius, bringing us another aspect of the enigmatic Maurice Ravel.

THE LYRE, Autumn Issue (special Ravel number) pages 4–7. 'The Strange Voyage of Maurice Ravel' by Dr Julius Newton and Mr Charles Pym

She was a young woman whose family had been music publishers in the city of Berlin for many generations. Her name was Marta Susskind. For a few years, her father, Herr Hans Susskind, had kept up a correspondence with a man named Maurice Ravel. This man wrote music of delight and beauty; music replete with the magic of the Orient and the sweet fierceness of Greek legend. He wrote songs, too: songs about strange voyages, and songs based on the Hebrew cadences of loss and death. He was a Frenchman; and whenever a letter arrived from him, with its elegant stamps, Marta knew that her father would be glad.

They kept up a spirited correspondence, those two; it was not merely a matter of Herr Susskind complimenting and Monsieur Ravel gracefully accepting. They spoke of art and literature as well as music; compared the Germanic spirit to the French one. The German wrote of the fervour and passion of German music and poetry, and mused as to why German painting and sculpture lagged behind those other two art forms. The Frenchman wrote of the three parallel streams of art he had grown with and into, poetry and music and painting. Susskind's letters were forceful and fervent, Ravel's elliptical and beautiful. Once, he had sent 'for the children' a most curious little creation—a tiny wooden mermaid sitting on a rock, set into a perfect glass oval on a shiny wooden base. When a cunningly concealed lever in the base was pulled, tiny waves lapped at the mermaid's feet, and she combed her hair. Over the years, the children played with it so often that, little by little, the mermaid's hand motions became jerky, the waves threatened to drown her. Marta was intrigued, but not surprised, that a grown man should have known to choose exactly the right toy to amuse children. When she was little, nothing about people surprised her. She was not looking for explanations, after all.

The years went by, the letters were still written, but more infrequently. Things were getting more difficult at home; Herr Susskind and his wife Emilia often looked worried.

One night, it all ended. Marta was eighteen, her brother thirteen, her sister eleven, when the family left Berlin forever, with nothing but the few clothes and belongings they had managed to carry with them. The world had changed around them; and now, Marta wanted explanations. But no-one would give them to her; for no-one could understand. On their hurried, secret way to France, Marta saw her father's face, and knew she could ask no questions. What would he have to say now about the Germanic spirit? What could he say, this man who had thought that the dark days were forever gone, that mankind was civilised now? He had admired the passion and fire of Wagner, his mystical fervour, without recognising the dark drumbeats underlying them. He had thought the German race to be epitomised by Beethoven, by Goethe, drawing order and sweetness and joy out of chaos and turbulence. He had been German. He could not be anything but German.

But now, in this extremity, he remembered the man who had inspired him with the 'Kaddisch'. He remembered his composed, beautiful letters. He took his family to Montfort l'Amaury, only to be told Ravel was at Saint-Jean-de-Luz, in the Basque country, his native place. Even this did not cause him to falter.

When Marta and her family first saw Maurice Ravel in person, he was sitting by a sunny window, at a table. He was wearing something soft, relaxed; perhaps even his beloved black silk pyjamas. But there was nothing déshabillé about him, nothing crushed, nothing that strayed from a particular kind of neat, almost dandy-like elegance. He was smooth, neat, as perfect as the curiosity he had sent the children, Marta thought. His hair was brushed smoothly, he was wearing beautiful leather slippers and silk socks on his feet, the pyjamas were not nightwear but more of a soft suit for the indoors. His eyes were deep-set, dark brown, ironic yet gentle; his face was a pale olive colour, not mobile, but not set either. A man at peace, thought Marta, not knowing that he was in the early stages of his illness, the illness that eventually robbed him not of ears but of voice, that cruelly allowed him to appreciate music, to even see music in his head, without ever being able to write it down.

There was nothing on the table in front of him but a single sheet of paper and a pencil. She thought about being in the presence of the composer of *Boléro*, of *Shéhérazade*, of *Daphnis et Chloé*, of the beautiful

Quatuor. And of the 'Kaddisch', of course. That was partly why they were there, because Herr Susskind remembered the 'Kaddisch'. He had not admired it particularly, back at home; but he had remembered it.

'You have done well to come here.' Mark's father and Maurice Ravel were talking, talking, and she was taking in the details of the room: the polished floors, the small pictures on the walls, the tables supporting a painstakingly arranged collection of objects. She thought it a strange place and him a strange man—a man-child—and for a moment, the thought frightened her. He would send them away, she knew. Letters were one thing, personal contact another, especially in those circumstances.

But they stayed. He made room for them in his careful, delicate way. He was never passionate about things, she would find. His eyes would not fill with tears, as her father's so easily did. But he made room. He asked questions for them, necessary questions about safe havens. Herr Susskind was not capable of those at that moment, nor Emilia.

He would walk with the children, down by the port. Once or twice, they went to Biarritz, to stroll on the promenade, and he told them stories about mermaids and sultans and Basque witches. With Marta, he was by turn shy and open, depending on what incarnation he saw her in—as woman, as child. He had many women friends, she knew, for they wrote to him, they came to see him often. He had many male friends too;

he was a man with a talent for friendship. But there was no-one to whom he seemed to have a particular attachment. Sometimes, Marta looked at him and saw not the world-famous composer, but a lonely figure: a man with a child's emotions, an adult sensibility, a necessity to wear a mask.

And then, one day, down by the edge of the sea, his eyes were different. And hers. The children were on the beach, playing. He did not say a word, or attempt to touch her, but she *knew*. There was something in the air between them, like a vibrating violin string. Something like music; something that could not be captured in words.

ARTS TODAY, February–March issue, page 3
'Discovery of Work Leads to New Ideas'

The recent discovery of a new work by the French composer Maurice Ravel (1875–1937) has sent shock waves through the music world.

The piano sonata, called *Le Gouffre* (*The Abyss*), was allegedly composed at a time of great personal hardship for the composer, and documents both his passionate love affair with the young German refugee Marta Susskind, and the onset of the brain illness that was to kill him finally four years later. It is likely to change ideas about the French composer, whose work has been described as 'charming, but without passion'.

The discovery was made by musician Charles Joseph Pym, who brought it to be authenticated by noted expert Dr Julius Newton. Dr Newton, who is well known as the author of several books on composers, said that the sonata appeared to be genuine.

'We are at present still conducting further tests on it,' he said. 'But so far there appears to be no doubt. This is the last, perhaps the greatest, of all Maurice Ravel's works.'

Page 4: Meredith Owens' interview with Charles Pym.

MEREDITH OWENS, 'The New Enigma'

A dapper, thin-featured figure with large dark eyes: that is your first impression of musician, composer and turner of established ideas, Charles Joseph Pym. Charles Pym has a calm, smooth face but hungry eyes, a face that puts the music lover irresistibly in mind of the man whose reputation he is changing: Maurice Ravel.

Charles Pym laughed gently when such a proposition was put to him.

'I am not obsessed with the man, you know! It is simply that people see what they want to see …'

Maurice Ravel's image is certainly changing, I suggested. How did he feel about that?

'Once again, people see what they want to see … perhaps now, they see something else, and that is good.'

It was an extraordinary story, I suggested, and fortuitous in the extreme.

'Life is extraordinary, and not always coherent, and often coincidental. It's only in books that we pretend it isn't so.'

How did he feel when he realised just what he had in his possession?

'At first, I felt stunned, of course. Then I realised what a real bombshell the whole thing actually was. That's when I knew I had to get expert help.'

Everyone loves a love story, a sad love story even more, I suggested. This discovery had certainly hit a nerve, and it was not only Ravel whose image was being changed. How had the discovery affected his own life?

'I live a quiet life, you know, and that hasn't changed much. I've been asked to write a few things, and I've even had an offer from a film company to tell my story. But it's not mine that's important; it's that of Ravel, of the music, of his love for Marta.'

People had suggested in the past that Ravel had no sexual feelings, I suggested. Did this prove that he did?

Charles Pym smiled. 'If you need proof, it does. I've never thought masculinity or femininity, the sexual things, can be as clearly defined as people think.'

But this new work had been described as having a 'quiet masculine strength'. Appropriate, perhaps, for an age when sabre rattling is no longer acceptable? Was Ravel an original Sensitive New Age Guy?

'If you like ... People are more complex than slogans though, you know. Who are we to judge?'

What made you choose Dr Newton, I asked, for corroboration of the papers?

'Because he is the foremost expert, of course ... But also I did not want to go to anyone too remote, too academic. Ravel was not only a brilliant musician, he also saw himself as a man of the people. He had distinct socialist leanings—one of his friends was Léon Blum in the Front Populaire—and he hated racism and pretension of any kind. He wanted people to love his work, not just respect it as some still, perfect thing. So it seemed to me that the person I chose had to be one Ravel would have approved of.'

But Ravel was such a private person, wasn't he? Wouldn't all this fuss have bothered him?

'You know, in the midst of his illness, one of Ravel's friends said to him, "But you have written so much already, your work is so beautiful, so complete." And he answered, in an anguished tone that chilled her, "I have written nothing! I have still so much more to write …" In this sonata, he has revealed much, much more of himself than we could ever have expected. And that is something that I feel sure he would have wanted to give the whole world.'

So we have cracked the enigma of Maurice Ravel? Isn't there something a bit final about it, a bit sad?

'The enigma is only in the eye of the beholder, you know,' he said, taking a flat silver box from his pocket, a box, which, to my astonishment, proved to contain carefully wrapped chewing gum. He offered me some, and I shook my head. But he meditatively took a piece out, unwrapped it, and put it daintily into his mouth. It came to me that here was another enigma.

★

February 18

Dear Julius,

        Thank you for your recent letter. Proofs of the book should be ready very soon. It will be no problem then to add The Society of French Music's endorsement of the manuscript, which you tell me is forthcoming. We are very excited by the look of the book, and I enclose a colour copy of the cover. What do you think? Let me know, soonest.

Also enclosed, an extremely interesting letter from Melody Records—it could be a great deal! Let me know very quickly on this too, as we could look at tying in the release of the CD and laser disc with the book—perhaps even packaging the whole together, or as a CD/book or CD/laser disc package. There's also the possibility of a CD-ROM package.

All the best,
Annalouisa Perugia
Managing Editor
Symphony Press

★

To Dr Julius Newton and Mr Charles Pym
c/o Symphony Press
(please forward)

Dear Dr Newton and Mr Pym,

        I have taken the liberty to write to you about the recent exciting discovery of a Ravel sonata which you have jointly made.

We at Melody Records would like to offer you the

best of terms in arranging a recording of this intriguing work. We understand that Mr Pym is himself a musician and pianist of some distinction, and would like to secure his services for the recording. We hope that Dr Newton would be interested in writing the cover notes. Our rates are extremely advantageous and we would like to look at entering into a contract with you as soon as possible—with release of the CD (and perhaps also a laser disc comprising a recording of the music, an introduction to the piece and an examination of Ravel's life and work, or even a CD-ROM package) to coincide with your press conference and the launching of the book.

We look forward to hearing from you with great interest.

Yours sincerely,
Louis Andrews
Managing Director
Melody Records

★

> University of the South West
> Bayonne
> France
> February 20

To Monsieur le Professeur Michel Simonin
Cher Michel,
        Here is the text I promised you. You can see it is extraordinary. Sorry it is late, but I have been kept very busy conducting my own research into it. I look forward to reading your comments.

Very best wishes to yourself, Cécile, and the family.

Julius Newton

★

Dear Dr Newton,
Professeur Simonin is away on three months' study leave in Java, and is incommunicado at present. When he returns, we will make sure he receives your communication.

Sandrine Delage (Madame)
for Prof. Simonin

EXTRACT OF TRANSCRIPT OF INTERVIEW, Radio National *Books Today*, May 5, with Julius Newton and Charles Pym. Interviewer: Maria Stricker

MS: An extraordinary moment indeed! Can you please describe to me, Dr Newton, your reaction on first sighting these documents?
JN: My first reaction was one of caution, Maria, because as I'm sure you know, such things don't often come our way! I have been working on my biography of Ravel for some time now, and when Mr Pym first mentioned the existence of these documents, I at once understood that we could be on to something very important.
MS: Will you explain to our listeners just why they were important?
JN: Well, you see, Ravel is is one of the most fascinating

of composers, precisely because his private life is very much a mystery. And of course, in our time, we understand just how great an impact a person's private life can have on his or her work—it does not explain or elucidate it, but it can offer extremely valuable clues, and sources of reflection. Also, I became very interested by the way in which a person's image, particularly that of a person in the public eye, as Ravel was, can become fixed at a certain point. That is, the image of that person is deemed to stay the same. It is only, I think, in our day, that we have begun to peel away the layers of previously hard-and-fast images of famous artists, composers, writers. These documents show that we have had an unnaturally fixed idea of Ravel for too long.

MS: Mr Pym, can you please describe the documents as you first saw them?

CP: They were in a box of papers left to me by a very great old friend of mine, a lady named Marta Susskind. She had never mentioned them before and, indeed, I was going to consign the whole lot to the fire, believing them to be intimate papers of hers, of no interest to anyone else, as naturally I am not a voyeur. But I chanced first upon this photo and then ...

MS: Could you please describe the photo which we have in front of us here?

CP: Certainly. It shows a young woman, rather plump, with straight dark hair, leaning on the arm of an older gentleman with deep-set eyes and white hair. They are on what appears to be the beach at Biarritz. On the back of the photo, there is a dedication: M.R. to M.S., 1934.

MS: And what else was there in that box, Mr Pym? It

certainly is a marvellous, romantic story, isn't it?

CP: The best stories are! In the box also were some sheets of music manuscript paper, filled with a composition, a sonata entitled *Le Gouffre* or, *The Abyss*, and a letter.

MS: And the composition is by Maurice Ravel?

JN: Yes! So far it appears to be absolutely genuine. It is an extraordinary piece, reminiscent of *Boléro* in some ways, yet more restrained, and more terrible too. It also features some jazz motifs with which we know Ravel was fascinated. But even more extraordinary is the knowledge that at this time of his life Ravel was indeed on the edge of an abyss, the terrible sickness which was to rob him of all powers of composition while not taking away his intelligence. This is the last, terrifying cry from the very lip of the abyss, a cry of anguish and love and madness which would put paid once and for all to the notion of Ravel as some kind of candied fop. You know, he once said, when it became apparent this horrible illness was threatening everything he cared for, 'I have not finished! I still have so much more to say!' Well, *Le Gouffre* says much, and says it in a way that affects everyone who hears it.

MS: And you think Marta was the inspiration?

JN: Well, I think she possibly stimulated this last, magnificent effort.

MS: And the letter? What was in the letter?

CP: It was a very powerful, short letter, expressing both anguish and joy ... You understand, Maria, that Dr Newton and I do not wish to divulge everything before the publication of our book.

MS (*laughs*): Of course, I understand! What can you tell us about Marta Susskind, Mr Pym, Dr Newton?

CP: You understand, I knew her only as a very old lady. She was my piano teacher for a long time, and I always loved going to her house, even though she was very strict. She had beautiful things in her house, especially a miniature mermaid, a beautiful little thing she once told me had been given to her as a present by a great man. Then she clammed up, and it was not until very recently that I understood who that had been.

MS: And this is the first time that a reciprocal sexual relationship with a woman—or indeed, anyone at all—has ever been suggested for the composer?

CP: Not the first time it's been suggested, no! His friend Remy Stricker—how extraordinary, Maria, that you share his surname—did say that once, due to a crossed line, he heard Maurice Ravel talk with a woman about a rendezvous he had failed to keep with her. And it has been suggested that he asked another friend, Hélène Jourdan-Morhange, to marry him, a proposal she rejected. He is also supposed to have known certain local prostitutes well, and Alma Mahler, a terrible gossip and spiteful with it, suggested she had seen him once with makeup on his face—an obvious homosexual reference. But till now, there has never been any proof or evidence of anything at all.

MS: Extraordinary, such discretion, in an age when we know everything a princess says to her supposed lover! Dr Newton, I understand you first met Mr Pym when he wrote a fan letter to you. What has it been like, collaborating with another person on this book?

JN: It has been simply marvellous! Charles and I understand each other completely, it's almost uncanny. He understands, too, a personality like Ravel's, for we are very alike. That reserve, that care is perhaps not a quality much admired these days, but it is, nevertheless, a clue to the man's greatness.

MS: Your books have been famous in the past for the way in which they look at composers and musicians as a whole, and not just personally or in terms of their work. How would you characterise the Maurice Ravel you are beginning to know?

JN: As a man of many parts. And yet as a man who refused to play a part. In there lies his enigma.

MS: An enigma which we are hoping to penetrate! Thank you both for a very interesting discussion, and we'll be looking forward to the publication of the book at the end of the month.

MUSICAL COURIER, April issue, page 2, 'Ravel in the Pays Basque' by Julius Newton

In some ways, the recent astonishing discovery of what must now be seen as Ravel's last work, the brilliant piano sonata *Le Gouffre* (*The Abyss*), is a reiteration of a well-known, yet neglected, strand in the composer's work. I refer of course to his Basque heritage, a heritage which sustained and nourished him throughout his life, despite his long residence in Paris.

The Basque motifs found in the sonata seem to point to the fact that Saint-Jean-de-Luz was the most likely place of composition of the work. This town, aptly named 'of light', is now a large and rather touristy place, but it is still charming, exhibiting the most accessible and delightful of Basque characteristics. Ravel himself was fond of drawing the distinction between the maritime and mountain people he came from, and the Mediterranean peoples, better known then, as now. Basques do not wear their hearts on their sleeves, he declared, yet they have deep, tenacious, strong hearts. Their music, their dress is elegant, not brash or obvious in any way. Perhaps if Ravel had not been born Basque, he would have had to re-invent himself as such?

Ravel spent much of his time in the house at Saint-Jean-de-Luz, which today still bears his name on the door. His sojourns in the Pays Basque were times of healing, of fun, of relaxing summers, but also of rediscovery, of plunging the self back into the sources of ancestry—into the culture of one of the oldest, if not the original, races of Europe. It is not surprising that in the time of despair and emotional stress that 1933 and thereafter represented for him, he took refuge there often. It is not difficult to imagine him sitting at his table in the sunshine, curtains blowing in the light sea breeze, as he composed this marvellous sonata. Here, his Basque heart—secretive, shy—had been awakened to the full possibilities of love. We can speculate that it was with Marta's help that he was able to make that superhuman effort, as the illness had already nearly robbed him of the facility of writing.

And the people of the Pays Basque, far from rejecting the man who was, after all, half-Parisian by now, claimed him as their own. Everywhere he went, in Biarritz, in Saint-Jean-de-Luz, in Bayonne, in Ciboure, in all those myriad, beautiful Basque towns and villages, people knew who he was, and loved him. 'Monsieur Ravel!' they would exclaim. And what if the work most on their lips was *Boléro*, what if Ravel had moved on since then? Always, with his sad, gentle smile, his deep eyes, he would accept their homage without arrogance.

That summer Marta and her family were there—the summer before the abyss—what was happening, in that fragrant little house near the sea? We may never know—but if we listen to that deep expression of Maurice Ravel's soul, we may learn, by instinct alone.

★

To the Editor,
Arts Today (April issue, 'Feminist Interpretation')

In all the furore about the new Ravel sonata, there is one silent witness—Marta Susskind herself. It is, of course, well known that male artists choose to use the women in their lives as muses. If Ravel was as ill as the evidence suggests, was it possible for him to write? Perhaps it was Marta Susskind herself who wrote the work, and had it passed off as Ravel's, knowing full well that a woman could never be accepted as a great composer. Has anyone checked this theory?

Sincerely,
Terri Summers

★

Dr Newton responds:

> As Ms Summers has so astutely pointed out, women were indeed the inspiration for many male artists, and some have even seen their own work tagged as that of their more famous companions. However, in this case we can be sure that Ravel, not Susskind, was the author of the work. There are certain signs which point to the utter authenticity of the work, signs which are being double-checked even now. Besides, there are no indications whatsoever that Susskind ever composed anything in her life.
>
> Julius Newton

★

You are invited to celebrate the launch of

The Pursuit of Beauty

The Life and Work of Maurice Ravel

by Julius Newton with Charles Pym

published by Symphony Press

To be launched by

the Hon. Sarah Ziegler,

Minister for the Arts

To be held at

the Silk Room

Hotel Pacific Glory

on May 28

at 6.30 p.m.

Drinks and light refreshments will be served

RSVP by May 2

Dear Julius,

Thank you for inviting us to the launch of your book and CD. We will, of course, be there! It has certainly become a big industry, hasn't it? Everywhere I look, I see mention of *Le Gouffre*. And that's here—imagine what it's like in France! But of course you know, having just been there.

Thank you, too, for your congratulations on my novel being short-listed for the Good Values prize. It is a bit of an embarrassment in a way, but at least it gives it lots of publicity, plus of course we couldn't sneeze at the money!

Did you know that Isabelle and I are at present collaborating on our first book together? You'll like this—it's for a series on the childhoods of famous musicians, artists and writers!

Looking forward to seeing you very soon, and I hope that you have thought further about the idea I mentioned to you a few weeks ago, about the possibility of me writing your biography. Of course it would interest people, Julius. And I think it would be very interesting for all of us …

Congratulations to you and Charles, and see you very soon.

Love from us all here,
Alex

★

> The University of the South West
> Bayonne
> France
> April 3

Dear Dr Newton,

It is with great regret that I inform you of the presumed death of our colleague, Professeur Michel Simonin, as a result of the unfortunate ferry accident off Java. His death leaves a huge space in all our lives, and especially in the field of research on our French composers.

Sadly,
Sandrine Delage (Madame)
Department of Music

TRANSCRIPT OF INTERVIEW, Radio National *Books Today*, May 24, with Julius Newton. Interviewer: Maria Stricker

MS: Well, Dr Newton, it's a pleasure to have you here with us again.
JN: Thank you, Maria. It's nice to be back.
MS: The launch of your book is very close now, isn't it?
JN: That's right. In four days' time.
MS: What are your feelings now?
JN: I'm excited, of course. I always am, when my books are published! Nothing's dimmed that pleasure.
MS: This particular book, though, has attracted an enormous amount of attention, hasn't it? Much more than usual?

JN: I'd like to think that my books always attract a lot of attention! Seriously, Maria, yes, this book's received massive attention, because I suppose it catches the imagination of people.

MS: There's been a real marketing drive for this book which I think hasn't happened to such an extent with your others. What do you feel about that?

JN: I feel quite comfortable with that. What I'm interested in doing is bringing the life and work of Maurice Ravel to as many people as possible. If you need marketing for that, so be it.

MS: And I understand that the book will be available as a package with a CD or other multimedia items?

JN: That's right. The things I've learnt about multimedia, Maria, are extraordinary. I feel like a babe in the woods in that respect. But I think it's a tremendous idea, for it brings the music to people, too, not just my—and Charles'—words. Although of course we want people to read those too!

MS: I understand that the book will be released in many countries and has already been translated into several languages. This must be very exciting for you.

JN: Of course, it's not the first time. My Beethoven and Grieg and Stravinsky books have also been sold in many countries. However, this is the first time that such a massive buy-in has occured. I think it will mean an enormous Ravel revival, all over the world.

MS: Your collaborator, Mr Charles Pym, is away in France at the moment, I believe. Will he be back in time for the big launch?

JN: Certainly he will! He wouldn't miss it for the world!

MS: Neither would I! Thank you so much, Dr Newton. And best of luck for the big day. And now I'd like to close this interview with an extract from a famous Ravel piece, *Tzigane*.

★

> Theodore Marais
> Paris
> May 25

Dear Dr Newton,

I am writing in haste as I was only just made cognisant of your need. It is difficult to make a thorough assessment of this work. Although technical aspects—paper type, pen type—appear to be consistent with an authorship in the 1930s, it is difficult to be sure that this is Ravel's writing. I note that the composer was ill at this time and so his writing undoubtedly changed and even markedly deteriorated. I have sent a photocopy of the work to an acquaintance of mine who works in the neurological field, and will send you results as soon as possible.

My advice is to be as cautious and conservative as possible. Could publication be delayed until we are absolutely sure?

Please accept my most cordial sentiments.

Theodore Marais

Recording of messages on Julius Newton's answering machine, May 26

> Dr Newton, I need to talk to you, as soon as possible. It's 10 a.m. I'll be at my number till 4.

> Dr Newton. Ring me. Please. If I am not here, leave a message.

> Dr Newton. It is rather late now. But if you ring me, perhaps we can talk.

FILE FOOTAGE, BOOK LAUNCH: HOTEL PACIFIC GLORY, *Behind the Arts*, SBS TV, May 28. Reporter: Sandra Makajev. Cameraman: Tolly MacMahon

(*Not all broadcast—extracts only shown on TV. A whirl of sound, people. A stage, people hushing. Minister for the Arts steps up to the stage. Flanking her are Symphony Press supremo, Sally-Ann Hawkins, and Melody Records MD Louis Andrews on one side. On her other side is Dr Julius Newton. The minister looks around, appears a little disconcerted, seems to be searching for someone. An official whispers something, she smiles.*)

Minister: Ladies and gentlemen, it is our very great pleasure to celebrate the launch of this magnificent book, and its accompanying, no less magnificent, CD. This project has been a labour of love for many people—the authors, the publisher, the recording company, as well as countless others. Not excluding, of course, the Arts Ministry! But I think it is especially a celebration of the life and work of that brilliant composer, Maurice Ravel.

(*Music fills the room. The sonata starts gently at first, then builds up. Then it is turned down, and the minister speaks again.*)

Minister: That, ladies and gentlemen, was the opening of this last, this newly discovered sonata, *Le Gouffre*, or *The Abyss*. It is a moving and intelligent piece, expressing lucidly both the joy of love and the bitterness of pain. In the book, the authors make it quite clear that the love Maurice Ravel and Marta Susskind bore for each other was cut off prematurely by Ravel's illness taking its toll. The composer had always said he did not want to impose the burden of his art on a lover; having discovered love, he did not wish to impose the intolerable burden of his sickness. And so he pushed Marta away. But not before he had composed this final, brilliant piece, which she undoubtedly transcribed for him, according to the authors' research. Ladies and gentlemen, this book is both a brilliant piece of deduction, and a moving tribute to a genius. It will, I believe, both inspire and entertain. It is a triumph for all concerned, and I heartily congratulate them all.

(*Claps, a few cheers. Julius Newton takes the stand. He smiles, his face is calm.*)

Julius Newton: Thank you, Minister, for your kind words. This is indeed a most marvellous occasion. At times we had to work against the clock to prove some of our points. It was indeed a difficult process, and my collaborator and I were on the point of despair many times. Yet always we felt this was a worthwhile project. In his absence, may I say that I would not have been able to do it without him. This is as much Charles

Pym's book as it is mine. Thank you all for coming—and here's to Maurice Ravel!

(*More applause. Then a disturbance, towards the back of the room. Someone is standing up, waving an arm.*)

Tom Rice here, freelance writer, Dr Newton. This is certainly an amazing story. What measures were taken to check its authenticity?

Newton: There were many tests conducted on both the work itself and the letter and photograph. Many experts were called in and ...

Rice: But what measures were actually taken? Didn't one of your experts die before he could prove anything?

Newton: You are referring to Professor Simonin? Yes, unfortunately that is the case. Nevertheless, we sent ...

Rice: Would you please look at this letter, Dr Newton? (*Holds up a piece of paper which he then passes up to Newton.*) Do you recognise this letter?

Newton: Certainly. It's the letter we received from the Association Musicale that ...

Rice: Would it interest you to know, Dr Newton, that the director of the Association Musicale, to whom I have sent a copy of this letter, declared it was never sent? That it is, in fact, a forgery?

(*A babble of voices. The officials with Newton look at each other.*)

Rice: Furthermore, would it interest all of you to know that Theodore Marais, a noted handwriting expert, urged caution about the documents? Or that there is no record whatsoever of any Marta Susskind in Berlin's civil records?

Newton: You must remember that many records were destroyed during the Second World War, and that ...

Rice: But the Susskind family were Jews, were they not? Is it not well known that exhaustive, neurotic records were kept on such families by the Hitlerian bureaucracy?

Newton: Perhaps, but many more were destroyed in the final conflagration. Also, my collaborator knew this lady, and she definitely existed, and ...

Rice: What about this then, Dr Newton? (*He holds up a small tape-recorder, and presses the switch. All listen, spellbound.*)

Rice: Would you not agree that that is Mr Pym's voice?

Newton (*looking ruffled for the first time*): Yes, I would, but where did you ...

Rice: Those are messages left on your answering machine, Dr Newton, some days before today. They sound urgent, do they not? Did you respond to them?

(*Newton says nothing.*)

Rice: You didn't, did you, because you knew what he was going to say, didn't you? That he'd got cold feet because he was afraid his hoax would be discovered!

(*Newton still says nothing. The group on the stage look at him, their faces betraying great agitation.*)

Rice: I submit to you, Dr Newton, that not only did you get taken in by a hoax, but that you grew to suspect it was one—yet did not try to stop it. Why, Dr Newton? I further submit to you that the so-called Ravel love letter included a passage from a story by Edgar Allan Poe, *The Narrative of Arthur Gordon Pym*, a story you knew well, or should have known well, if you had looked at the influence of Poe on Ravel. In fact, I submit that your collaborator, or should I say your accomplice, began to be frightened and wanted to stop matters, but that you refused. What do you say to that?

Newton (*getting up*): I have nothing to say, except to my lawyer.

Rice: Wait, Dr Newton. One further question. Did you know definitely that the whole thing was a hoax by the time you received the supposed Association Musicale letter, or before then?

(*Newton is helped off the stage, pursued by the media, and disappears through a side door.*)

THE NATIONAL HERALD, May 29, page 1, 'A Clever Hoax'

Copies of the recently published Ravel biography, *The Pursuit of Beauty*, have had to be recalled following sensational allegations that some of the material published was a forgery.

The photo, letter and sonata manuscript comprising the so-called 'Ravel papers' have been described by well-known investigative journalist, Mr Tom Rice, as a 'clever hoax'. The photo, Mr Rice revealed, was cleverly constructed using the latest digital technology, while the documents, including the sonata, were simple forgeries.

Mr Rice, who revealed the doubts about these documents at a dramatic press conference on Tuesday, has named his source as one of the book's authors, Charles Joseph Pym.

Mr Rice said that although the work in question, *Le Gouffre* (*The Abyss*), and accompanying documents gave the impression of authenticity, they were in fact created by Mr Pym, an accomplished musician with a varied and colourful career.

He said the whole story showed the glaring deficiencies in authenticating works.

'It is all quite hopelessly ad hoc,' he said. 'There are simply not enough checks and balances, and things are done in too much secrecy, as people hope to steal marches on each other. For instance, the letter [the text of which is reproduced below] contained a well-known passage from a story by Edgar Allan Poe. That should have alerted Dr Newton at once. And if not, why not?'

Mr Pym first came to Dr Newton, the book's main author, with the papers, some months ago.

Mr Rice said that Dr Newton accepted their provenance almost immediately.

'He was just so set on the whole thing, he couldn't see the wood for the trees,' he said.

It is not known if any criminal charges are to be laid, although there are expectations that both the publisher and record company involved will sue the authors.

However, Mr Pym is uncontactable, according to Mr Rice, and Dr Newton is not answering media questions.

Police said yesterday that unless a formal complaint was lodged, they would not be looking for Mr Pym.

Text of 'Ravel' letter (with passages lifted from Poe story in italics)

Before ... *the darkness materially increased, I rushed into the embraces of the cataract, where a chasm threw itself open to receive me*. The abyss yawned, I would be in it, all senses, all faculties lost.

But after, ah! I can dissimulate no further. You, whom I have waited for, so patiently, so impatiently, on the edge of the abyss ... Tenderly, I have searched for you. Tenderly, I have found you. I will never let you go, now.

M.

THE NATIONAL HERALD, May 30, page 4, 'The Strange Voyage of Julius Newton' by Tom Rice

It is always a sad thing when a respected public figure stoops to the indignity of deception. It is even more so when that figure was one of your own pantheon of heroes. Such a one was Julius Newton, subtle biographer of, among others, Beethoven, Grieg, Stravinsky and Purcell. And would-be biographer of one of the most elusive of musical geniuses, Maurice Ravel.

I first began to have intimations as to Dr Newton's voyage into deception when I received a phone call from a man calling himself Charles Joseph Pym.

I will repeat those first words of his verbatim.

'Those Ravel papers,' he said. 'They're a hoax. And Newton knows it.'

Well, I had heard of them—who hadn't? But I was frankly disbelieving until Pym told me the whole sorry tale, a tale of complacency, of self-deception and finally of closing eyes to fraud—and worse.

Pym said, sorrowfully, 'I gave him many clues that things were not as they seemed. I tried to make him submit the papers to rigorous testing, but always there was something which stopped him. One expert most fortuitously died off Java; the Association Musicale never received a letter which was supposed to have been sent; the cautious opinion of yet another was discounted. And the fact that the so-called love letter contained straight liftings from one of Poe's stories—he chose to ignore that. Julius Newton never wanted to give up the helm of his ship of self-deception, heading straight for the abyss. His tragedy was not pre-ordained. At any time, any time, he could have pulled back, looked properly. But he chose not to.'

He chose not to—what a terrible phrase. What next, one wonders, for Julius Newton? As with other experts—those taken in by the Haydn manuscripts, the Hitler diaries, to name but two—his career and reputation are on the line. This is indeed a horrible tragedy, for it not only throws the Ravel research into disrepute, but also all the rest of Dr Newton's work.

THE NATIONAL HERALD, **Editorial, June 1, 'Fall From Grace'**

While one may have sympathy for Ravel Hoax victim Dr Julius Newton, it is difficult to sustain in the face of his silence before his accusers. Those of us who grew up with Dr Newton's brilliant musical biographies will be saddened by the fall of a literary giant. A Greek tragedy has unfolded before us.

DAILY TIMES, Editorial, June 1

The silence of Dr Julius Newton speaks louder than any words. Innocence would by now have been loudly proclaimed, if it could be. It is a sad day indeed when you see that those who set themselves up as the elite fail to take the most elementary of precautions. If Dr Newton had been a factory worker, or an office worker, he would have been sacked for his dangerous disregard for the truth. As it is, he has brought down well-deserved ridicule on the literary and musical establishments—and he has destroyed himself.

★

May 30

Dear Dr Newton,

I am instructed to advise you that Symphony Press has decided not to proceed with legal action against you. However, all advance moneys for the publication *The Pursuit of Beauty* must be repaid. Please telephone this office at the above number to request further information.

Yours sincerely,
Colin Duckton
Duckton, Jones and Rizzi
Solicitors

★

Dear Dr Newton,
           I regret to inform you that the *Musical Courier* is herewith returning your article, 'The Death of Ravel'. In the circumstances, it was felt it would be inappropriate for us to publish it. Regretfully, we do not anticipate commissioning further articles from you in the near future.

Yours sincerely,
Amber Rose (for the Editor, *Musical Courier*)

★

FAX TO JULIUS NEWTON
FROM GEOFFREY ZAUBER, EDITOR, *THE LYRE*
May 30, 2.42 p.m.

Dear Julius,
           I am deeply sorry but my publisher just will not allow me to take on board anymore of your articles—at least till all this business is sorted out. And I hope it will be, soon.
    Sorry again, Julius. And keep in touch.

Sincerely,
Geoffrey Zauber

★

FAX TO JULIUS NEWTON
FROM THE *MESSENGER*—WHERE THE TRUTH IS TOLD!
June 1, 9 a.m.

Dear Dr Newton,

      Here at the *Messenger* we are sure that you have your own story to tell. Could one of our staff call on you and discuss terms for a possible exclusive?

Yours sincerely,
Mario di Maggio (Editor)

REDIAL 10 a.m., 11.30 a.m., 2 p.m., 3 p.m., 3.30 p.m.
FAX MACHINE NOT RESPONDING AFTER 3.30 P.M.

★

FAX TO JULIUS NEWTON
FROM *BEHIND THE HEADLINES* CURRENT AFFAIRS PROGRAMME
June 1, 10.15 a.m.

Dear Dr Newton,

      We are preparing a feature programme on the affair of The Ravel Papers and would like to ask you for exclusive rights to your side of the story. We will also be contacting Mr Tom Rice and, through him, Mr Charles Pym. Please contact us urgently at the above number.

William Shaw
Producer

★

June 2

Dear Ms Newton,

I received your letter yesterday and was most offended by its implications.

No, I did not seek out the story; Mr Pym rang me. This was definitely a story in the public interest, and I make no apology whatsoever for following my craft. I see no reason to disbelieve Mr Pym; the case he presented to me was most compelling. It is certainly sad.

I most certainly have no animus against Dr Newton and in fact would have preferred this thing not to have happened at all. But you must understand, Ms Newton, it is the job of the journalist to seek the truth and to publish it if it is in the public interest.

I am, of course, willing to hear Dr Newton's side of the story, but as he has refused to speak to me, I do not know what else I can do.

I regret I cannot inform you as to Mr Pym's whereabouts.

Yours sincerely,
Tom Rice

★

June 3

Dear Dr Newton,

As you know, we convened for our final selection meeting on Friday. In view of recent events, we have decided that it would not be appropriate for us to offer you the keynote speech, as was originally discussed.

We are sure you will understand our position.

Yours sincerely,
Marisa Beaumont
For the Committee
First City Arts Festival

★

June 3

Dear Dr Newton,

I regret to inform you that your services will not be required this year for the judging of the Premier's Non-Fiction Prize. As you know, the composition of our panel changes frequently and in the circumstances it was felt you would perhaps not wish to continue on it.

Yours sincerely,
Kieran Burke
Department of the Premier and Cabinet

★

June 5

Dear Dr Newton,

In view of recent events, it is felt that the honorary doctorate which the university had intended to bestow on you might be seen as inappropriate. We therefore regretfully inform you that the investiture will not take place.

Yours sincerely,
(Professor) James Di Angelo
Head, Arts Faculty
East Coast University

★

He is sitting alone by the open window, the sun slanting gently onto him, the soft breeze bringing him the sounds of the fishing port. At his elbow little tables, with carefully placed, curious objects on them. He is wearing something soft, relaxing; perhaps even his beloved black silk pyjamas. But there is nothing undressed, unthinking about him; nothing crushed. His white hair is brushed smoothly, he is wearing beautiful leather slippers and silk socks on his feet; the pyjamas are not exactly nightwear but more of a soft suit for the indoors. His eyes are deep-set dark brown, ironic, yet gentle; his face is of a pale olive colour, not mobile, but not set either. A man at peace, you might think, seeing him sitting there, at the table, a single sharpened pencil and a page of manuscript paper in front of him. But inside his brain a storm is raging, a livid flash of maddening cruelty. A cruelty that allows him to hear the music, to know it, yet be unable to express it. He pulls the paper towards him, plunges the pencil at it, and begins to write, slowly, painfully, frustratingly, the tears damming at the back of his eyes.

Part 3

THE ABYSS

one

Dear Docteur Newton,

You may know that I was an assistant of Professeur Simonin's before his tragic death last year. I was helping him to compile his research work on French composers, particularly Maurice Ravel. You know, of course, that Professeur Simonin was in Indonesia to research the influence of gamelan music heard at the 1889 Paris World Fair on composers such as Ravel and Debussy. Of course, you know Ravel was very young—only fourteen—at the time, but Professeur Simonin was sure certain traces of this exotic music are present in his later work.

While engaged in this research, he found out the names of some of the musicians who had played at the fair, and found that one of them had actually stayed at the home of a certain Cyprien Baudel, who was later a well-known musician in Biarritz. It fell to me to find the Baudel family, and to conduct an interview with its sole surviving member, Mademoiselle Mathilde Baudel, who presently lives in Saint-Jean-de-Luz.

I began my interview with questions about the Javanese musician, a young man named Sujono, but as you will read, we rapidly passed on to other things. I felt you should have a copy of this interview, as I believe it shows that the so-called 'hoax' that you were so tragically subject to, was, in fact, double-layered. I have also taken the liberty of sending the copy of the sonata which you sent to Professeur Simonin to be analysed by certain experts who have worked for us before. I will, of course, let you know their findings immediately.

I hope you will not mind my writing to you in this fashion. I know Professeur Simonin considered you to be both a good friend and a marvellous writer, with a clarity and precision that has won you so many readers in my home country. I know he would not want you to be the victim of such a cruel deception. I would have written to you before, but I am afraid that my own grief at the Professeur's death has been my chief preoccupation for some time, and it is only lately that I have returned fully to the work in which we were engaged. I think you will be pleased to know that it will continue.

You will notice that the enclosed interview is rather more than a mere transcript. Professeur Simonin insisted that his research assistants sketch in setting and so forth, and make our own observations. He did not believe in objective observers, and felt it was better if we were honest about our impressions, though he certainly didn't accept them at face value. It is one of the reasons I will so miss the Professeur; unlike so many of his colleagues, there was never a dull day with him.

Please accept my most cordial and respectful greetings.

Sandrine Delage (Madame)

TRANSCRIPT OF INTERVIEW OF MADEMOIS-ELLE MATHILDE BAUDEL, SAINT-JEAN-DE-LUZ, by Sandrine Delage

I am in Saint-Jean, the town where Ravel himself had a house. Later, after I have visited the old lady, Mathilde Baudel, I will take a walk to Ravel's house. But for the moment, I am going very slowly along the narrow, deep streets that lead down to the old port, where I will park. It is fairly quiet in Saint-Jean, this not being the tourist season yet, but still the old town is not made for modern traffic.

Mathilde Baudel's flat is small, very small, but it fronts on to a view of the port, and the exciting, disturbing scents of the fishing boats come wafting in through the open windows. Her maid has set a small table for morning coffee: a gold coffee pot and cream jug, fine gold and white cups of a china so fine it looks almost translucent. There is a cake from Dodin's on a glass dish; a work of jewel-like perfection, the name slashed carefully across its top.

'Madame, I am Sandrine Delage. I spoke to you on the telephone about ...' She stays seated, she looks old, very old, her hair quite white, thin, but bravely curled. Her face is very white too, very lined; her eyes pale and rather watery behind her plain gold-rimmed glasses.

'*Mademoiselle* Baudel, please! But you may call me Madame. I know who you are. You want to talk about Monsieur Sujono. And Monsieur Ravel.' The old woman's voice does not match her appearance: it is sharp, brisk, and very bright.

I nod. She folds her hands, her eyes suddenly staring off into the distance.

'Of course, I do not remember Monsieur Sujono. My father met him when he was a young man. He had gone, like so many, to have a look at the Paris World Fair. It was a marvellous occasion, he said, especially for a boy from the south who was mad about art and music and literature. It was there he met Monsieur Sujono, who was, I believe, a native of Java. He had come with other members of his orchestra to play the strange compositions they call *gending*, musical pieces for gamelan. My father said it was extraordinary! He had never heard such sounds before, as indeed had very few. The freedom, the strange tonalities, the haunting quality of the music transfixed him, as it transfixed others—including, I believe, Debussy, Satie, and a very young Ravel. French composers, you see, had been exposed to what was, for them, the exoticisms of the Russians, but in these Javanese and Balinese musicians, and in the Hindustani and North African singers who were there at the fair, for the first time many saw the world of possibilities that lay before them. I believe it was a seminal experience for many of them. I remember, actually, my father talking about it years later. That such music could be outside the strict classical bounds of tonality, yet be so strictly tied to a tonal centre that is repeated and grown upon: that was a truly astonishing realisation for many of them.'

'And Sujono ...' I prod gently. She looks at me with a slightly impatient expression, and went on as if I hadn't spoken. 'Of course, it was not only musicians who were influenced. Artists were bowled over by their encounter with Japanese and Chinese art; theatre people with the craft of the Annamites; literary people with the wealth of symbolism to be got from this veritable caravanserai of cultural riches. I often think, these days, of how innocent they all were. It is hard for you young people to imagine, in this time when the world knows all the world's business, how liberating, yet frightening in a sense, was that glimpse into other worlds. For the creative spirits it was a new source of inspiration; for the rest of us, it was an acquiring of new, rich, exotic tastes that nevertheless did not penetrate deep down. So it was with my father. He became friendly with Sujono, and for a few days they saw the capital together; and he took Sujono home to meet his Parisian relatives (my aunt lived there at the time) and they exchanged addresses. They did, in fact, correspond for some time, but I believe Sujono died relatively young.'

This is my cue. 'Madame, no doubt you know that we are researching the influence of such musicians on our own composers, and ...'

'Yes, of course, of course,' she says impatiently. 'I was getting to that. My father spoke quite often of his conversations, such as they were, with Sujono—for the young man spoke no French, only Javanese and Dutch, and my father spoke no Dutch or Javanese, that goes without saying. But he knew German quite well, and they got along with that. Sujono said that his orchestra had been introduced to some 'French musicians', but he couldn't exactly remember their names. But my father, who was often at the fair, said that he was sure he'd spotted many luminaries, including Debussy, in the crowd around the gamelan players. And once, he'd glimpsed a small, intense-eyed, elegant *petit jeune homme*, and he was always sure it was Monsieur Ravel. Especially as, in later life, my father came to know him reasonably well. Of course, you know my father, in his day, was considered to have one of the best music shops in France, outside of Paris, as well as being a well-known musician. Monsieur Ravel, on his frequent visits to his mother's native region, patronised my father's shop in Biarritz. He was an extraordinary man: so delicate, yet never diffident; shy, yet friendly. He was a man who inspired extraordinary affection; though he kept his private life well hidden, and we never knew if he had any particular *objects d'amour*, as you might say.'

She looks at me rather mischievously. 'It has been rumoured Monsieur Ravel fell in love with a ballerina once, when the Ballets Russes were at their height,' the old woman says. Her eyes are on the past, her voice is softer, turned inwards. 'But nothing was proven. It's also been said that when he died a secret cabinet was discovered at his house in Montfort l'Amaury, a cabinet stuffed full of the most incredible letters, which have disappeared into the Bibliothèque Nationale. I don't know, it's all hearsay. But I do know he had many friends. He was a loved man. He had been a deeply loved child—his parents were intelligent, imaginative people who had made the childhood of himself and his brother Edouard a marvellous thing indeed. He was loved by his friends, by his family. His brother Edouard and he stayed close till his death.

'And let me tell you, Madame, as an adult he was a wonderful friend for a child too! I have seen him leave a group of important adults to get down on the floor and play with a group of children. He understood games of imagination, Madame! Oh yes, he did. Many's the time I have seen him, his face as serious as any of ours, become somebody other than what he was—a king, a dragon, a fairy, a mermaid. Oh, he had a gift, Madame! He had lovely things in his house, things we were allowed to touch—they were not just for looking at, like most of our parents' things were— cunning little objects, clockwork creatures and intricate little houses, scenes trapped under glass ... And he would bring presents, such lovely presents ... I remember once he brought me a glass paperweight in the shape of a chest, with what looked like pirates' treasure embedded inside. I had it for years, for years, until my brother broke it, one day.'

Subconsciously, her eyes flash, her nostrils tighten, as she remembers the anger, the grief of that day.

She motions impatiently at me to pour the coffee, and continues.

'Yes, I sometimes think our Monsieur Ravel was a child trapped in an adult's body. He had the musical sensibilities of maturity, yet the imagination of a child. Maybe it was that happy childhood of his. That is why, I think, his music has not been seen as important as, say, Debussy's. He is seen as too childlike, too delicate in his approach. People these days—those days too— want loud passion, declarations of intention. They accuse him of being artificial, but do you know what he said once about that? "Hasn't it occured to them that one can be artificial by nature?"'

'But Madame, I ...' I begin, daring rather foolishly to interrupt, as she stares impatiently at me.

'For the expression of Ravel's own ideas on music,' she says quellingly, 'I draw your attention to the famous interview with David Ewen in *Etudes* [extract enclosed]. How could one say Monsieur Ravel did not understand emotion? It was simply that he despised the shouting of it from the rooftops, as the Wagnerian disciples were so fond of doing. And look where the spirit of Wagner got Germany! Strangely enough, Monsieur Ravel's literary tastes were almost diametrically opposed to his musical genius: he loved the self-conscious theatrics of horror perpetrated by Edgar Allan Poe and Baudelaire and the like. It is interesting, no? The disordered, hectic rush of Poe's prose, however, masks an artifice as contrived as it is odd. And similarly, you could say that the beauty of Monsieur Ravel's music, like Mozart's, masked the extreme emotional sensitivity at its heart. And that was what ordinary people responded to. They weren't fooled by perfection; they responded with their hearts, even if too many of the critics didn't.'

She looks at her hands for a moment, sighing. Of course, at this point I cannot resist asking her a question about the scandal that has broken over the forgery of the Ravel sonata, which all the newspapers have covered so recently. She looks shrewdly at me. 'I know, my girl! You want to know if there's any connection with this Charles Pym. I never did hear of a Pym, or ...'

'Marta Susskind?'

'No, no, not that either. But this sonata that Pym is supposed to have written—yes, yes, my dear, of course I keep in touch with all that's happening, music was my life, you know—I do wonder. Of course, sonatas are not written anymore. They are seen as old-fashioned, like fables and sonnets.'

'Oh, but they aren't! They are being revived now, and ...'

'There was no mention of the kind of manuscript paper used. That could be a way of checking for sure.' She fixed me with a brilliant gaze, her eyes no longer watery. 'You know, of course, about that? Manuscript paper differs slightly from country to country in terms of dimension, thickness and spacing.'

She smiles, and sips the coffee I have poured. 'It would certainly have been so in the days I am talking about. But that is by the by. What is more important, of course, is the quality of the music, the signature, if you like. Maurice Ravel's work is very peculiar to himself—there is a charm, a wistfulness, yet a certain tautness too, a litheness that often escapes the attention of critics. And if your sonata is orchestral, or partly so, there is another clue. Monsieur Ravel was a great orchestrator: he used the orchestra as if it were one musical instrument. Do you understand? That unity, that sense of purpose, that perfection: not one note too many or too few, that is his signature.'

'But it has been shown to be a fraud,' I say regretfully, wanting now more than ever for *Le Gouffre* to be real.

'That is as may be,' she says, the light going from her eyes. 'Perhaps we may cut the cake now? And mind, I do not want any crumbs on the carpet.'

'Madame, when you knew Monsieur Ravel, did you know of any German Jewish refugees who had stayed with him?'

'There were many such came calling,' she says, taking a forkful of cake. She puts it in her mouth and a look of great satisfaction comes over her face. 'Ah, some things don't change, thank goodness. Now, yes. There were many such. People used to knock at his door in Montfort l'Amaury, just because they'd heard his music, loved it, wanted to tell him so. And, of course, he loathed all racism, you know. He thought it showed stupidity and lack of imagination. But I don't remember specific families. Certainly not a Marta Susskind.'

I look at her, seated there frail and bird-like in her chair, her cheeks bulging with cake, and feel a kind of terror that one day I will be like this—imperiously commanding strangers and blow-ins from the past, impervious to any pleasure save memory or cake.

It is nearly lunchtime by the time I get ready to go. Mademoiselle Baudel has made it quite plain that I needn't expect to stay for lunch, that she needs her nap and that she has ordered in some delicate confections for her meal which she does not want to share. So I get up carefully, filled with wonderful cake and still held in the spell of the world she has conjured up. A woman comes through from the kitchen, and silently she gathers up the cups and plates. I wonder if she's been listening, and whether she's heard this story before. Mademoiselle Baudel is sitting right back in her chair, her eyes closed. It does not seem she will notice my going. Only when I have murmured my goodbyes and I am moving towards the door does she suddenly open both eyes—bright and sharp as ever—and say, 'There was one thing that jolted my memory after I read that rather incautious piece Monsieur Newton wrote about Monsieur Ravel's supposed relationship with this Marta Susskind. That mermaid in the glass, I remember her.'

She smiles secretively at my stunned face. 'But it was not given to a Marta Susskind. A girl I knew, older than me, the daughter of one of my parents' friends. She told me, as a secret, that Monsieur Ravel had given it to her. Maybe that was true, maybe it wasn't.'

Her pause is theatrical. She looks at me from under her eyelashes, smiling. 'Her name was Augustine Bernard. I don't know where she is now, but I understand she met an Australian soldier after the war.'

ENCLOSURE: Extract from interview with Ravel by David Ewen, in *Etudes* (1928)

... great music must ever come from the heart. Music that is made with technique and intellect is not worth the paper it is written on. This has always been my argument against the so-called modern music of the younger rebellious composers. It is the product of their heads, not their hearts. *First they devise complicated theories, then they write music to satisfy these theories.* [my italics: S. Delage]

... I do not understand the arguments of composers who tell me the music of our times must be ugly because it expresses an age that is ugly. Why does an ugly age need expression? And what is left of music if it is robbed of its beauty? Theories are all very nice, but a composer should not write his music by theories. He should create musical beauty straight from the heart and feel intensely what he composes.

★

Dear Madame Delage,

                I am very grateful for the trouble you have taken in sending me the material on Ravel. It was very interesting indeed. However, I do not wish to enter into correspondence on the matter, as the whole issue, as I am sure you will understand, has been quite painful for me.

Cordial respects,
Julius Newton

★

Dear Docteur Newton,

Since my last letter, I have received word from our expert as to the provenance of the Gouffre sonata. He is persuaded that on the evidence he has before him, the sonata is genuine. He would like to see the original manuscript, if possible, if you have it, as I understand you do. In fact, I am preparing to travel to Australia to see you—I am intending to arrive there next month, and will let you know full details very soon. Please, Docteur Newton, allow me to do so. I believe we owe it to the memory of both Ravel and Professeur Simonin, not to speak of your own reputation. I firmly believe you have been the victim of a monstrous deception, a deception which I intend to expose.

Respectfully yours,
Sandrine Delage (Madame)

★

Chère Madame Delage,

It really is too kind of you to take such an interest in my sad little case, but I am not sure if anything I can say or do will change matters in any event. My dear lady, it is very touching to read of your belief in me, and I could not be so churlish as to refuse to see you. However, I only have a copy of the sonata—Mr Pym took the original with him. I do, however, for some reason, have the original of the sonata's title-sheet, which may be of some use.

Cordial good wishes,
Julius Newton

★

Dear Docteur Newton,

                      I arrive in Sydney on Saturday the 4th. I hope to see you the following day, Sunday, if that is convenient. I am looking forward very much to meeting you.

Best wishes,
Sandrine Delage

two

Django Reinhardt on the radio, the car bouncing along the narrow road, the wind shaking the trees into silver paroxysms: Roxane drove steadily, both hands firmly on the wheel. Beside her, Julius sat with his eyes closed, apparently dozing. Out of the corner of her eye she could see his right leg twitching a little in its impeccable knife-edge trouser, and the sight made her unaccountably sad. In the midst of the nightmare of the last few months, Julius had persisted in his orderly habits, the delicate care of his clothing, his person. In the beginning, when the story was still hot, still a great occasion for the sniggering due to a fallen hero, newspapers and magazines had published articles about him, stressing these very traits, as if they were in themselves laughable. After one disastrous interview Julius had not spoken to the media again, but the damage had been done.

'Django was still very much a Romany, even in the midst of the glamour of his new world,' the announcer said at the end of a song. 'He never lost those Romany traits, the very same that fired his guitar: fire, passion. But yet there was a delicacy of tone ...'

Roxane turned the sound down. She didn't want to hear the pontificating that went on. Let the music speak for itself.

'I was listening,' Julius said, opening one eye. 'Turn it up, please.'

'I thought you were asleep.' Roxane was annoyed to find herself speaking resentfully. Julius did not answer. He opened the other eye and, leaning forward, twiddled the knob so that the sound rose. The man had finished talking, and, instead, there was the music: Stephane Grappelli's quicksilver violin and Django's bouncy guitar. Simple, innocent, happy music— it was hard to remember that much of it had been composed just before and during the Second World War.

Julius' fingers tapped gently on his knee. He said, 'Just there, see, there's a motif very similar to the one in the new Ravel piece.'

That's what they don't understand, Roxane thought in sudden despair. They wonder why Julius is still so jaunty, why he is 'gallant', as they put it, while laughing behind their hands. Thank God he still has enough sense of self-preservation not to tell them he still believes in it all, despite everything. That was why they were on their way down to the city, so that Julius could embark on his campaign to validate something everyone else—except that silly Frenchwoman,

Sandrine Delage— knew to be a hoax. Julius knew what she thought, and he knew what Alex thought, but he closed his eyes and his ears, persisting in a cause which could only bring him more grief.

Wasn't it enough that he had been made into a laughing stock? Wasn't it enough that, even now, vultures in the shape of revisionist critics were getting ready to plunge their beaks into his earlier works? Wasn't it enough that he had lost his income, his credibility, even his creativity? He had not lifted his pen to write since the dreadful fiasco; it was almost as if he were under a spell. He had been done like a dinner, and the most shocking thing of all was to realise how few friends he really had. All those talks, those conferences, those meetings, those interviews had vanished like dew in the morning. The same people who had praised Julius Newton now excoriated him, or intimated they'd always known there was something not quite sound about him.

There had been utter silence from those who had been taken in, just like Julius, by that creature Pym. Except for a rather nice but ineffectual letter from the editor of *The Lyre*, Geoffrey Zauber. He'd been genuinely regretful; but not strong enough to really defend Julius in public. And Alex, of course—dear Alex. Even Julius had been moved by his nephew's loyalty, she knew that, though of course he'd never say it. Poor Julius, poor, stiff, unhappy Julius ...

'Django kept his head down during the Occupation, though the Germans knew better than to touch him or his family,' the man's fruity tones went on. 'He kept playing music and composing, and kept clear of political involvement of any kind, though he watched over his family like a hawk. Django was greatly influenced during this time by the American greats of jazz and, after the war, was thrilled to meet them. People who met him during this time speak of his mysterious character, the notion that he ...'

'There was nothing mysterious about him,' Julius declared, turning the radio down. 'He just played music, that's all, and loved it. Django was a simple character. Unlike—'

'How about we stop for a moment?' Roxane interposed quickly. She simply could not bear to hear another word about Maurice Ravel. It was odd, really—Julius had become more and more obsessed by the composer, though he never spoke of Pym at all.

And yet it was Pym who was truly the composer of that piece, Roxane thought angrily. It did exercise her mind, the notion of Pym: why would someone do a thing like that? Why would someone, with such obvious talent, waste it on a hoax? It must be because the man was so hollow; he had no creative centre in himself, but must rob it from others. There had been that sense of a disconnected self with him, she remembered. An emptiness at his very centre, a cold malice. An abyss, just like the bloody piece of music he had written.

But Julius did not seem to ask himself such questions. And when she had asked them herself, a few weeks ago, he had merely looked at her and said, 'That is of no consequence.' He refused to see that he should have defended himself against the man; he was completely against trying to find out anything about him. Of course, now she knew it was because he had managed to convince himself of the sonata's authenticity. Thanks to that woman. Although perhaps it was more due to his overweening self-belief, even now. Thank God none of the journalists had ferreted that out. Or the Calvary would have been even more horrible.

She turned off the road into a picnic area. 'Time to stretch legs.' Julius said it with satisfaction, as if it had been his idea. Watching him unfold himself from his seat and open the door, she thought of her years away, the years in the States with Seth, and cursed herself for coming back. Julius did not need her, as she had persuaded herself. He had never needed anyone.

Seth had not understood at all why she would leave the country that had become her home to go back to an uncle he had never even met. She could not tell her son that she felt a terrible yearning to return, not to Julius, but to this place, this country, this strange, unsatisfactory land that lodged itself under your skin like one of its own grass seeds. Seth would have been offended, aggrieved even—he had been a warm, loving, overwhelming child, and was the same as a man. He thought that all you had to do to exorcise unfinished business was to talk of it exhaustively, analysing every nuance. Even if he could not fully understand Roxane's wish to see Julius again, at least it fell within his scale of things people did. He'd told her that she was looking at re-inventing her past, and she had nodded, and smiled ruefully, because it seemed the easiest thing to do. But inwardly she had thought, Oh my Seth, my dear little Seth. He could never understand how she could carry a kernel of coldness within her, a coldness that had been in her since Alexander's death, many years ago. He could not understand how similar she was to Julius, how the close, warm habits she had developed since living in the States were falling away from her as if they had never existed.

With a sigh, she got out of the car. Yes, Seth, she told him silently, you wouldn't have believed me if I'd told you I was coming back for this country. And you might have been right. For when she saw her brother, tremors of unexpected feelings, feelings dormant long since, had made themselves felt. Pity, irritation, admiration, love, anger, even forgiveness: Julius inspired all of these. Talking to Alex the other day, on the phone, she had found herself saying, 'He is breaking his heart and I can't just watch it happening.' She had been horrified at that: had all her careful irony come to nothing? She watched him now, walking briskly around the picnic area, an elderly man who did not show his age till you saw him up close. And her eyes filled with the kinds of tears Julius himself would never shed. Had Pym really done the impossible—crushed Julius' spirit, so that he could no longer distinguish truth from fiction? He had always been such an ironist, such a subtle observer of the human condition. Had Pym killed that in him? It would appear so.

Not for the first time, Roxane felt real hatred towards Pym, who could come and destroy a life, a spirit, a family, a reputation, and get away with it. Yet had he? Who would now ever listen to any compositions he might write without thinking of his hoax? Who now would take him seriously? He had destroyed his own life just as effectively as he had destroyed Julius'.

In the early days of revelation, she and Alex had wanted to track him down, to make him face what he had done. But Julius had refused to co-operate, refused even to give them Pym's last contact point. He had said it was of no consequence: the man was a liar, and anyone could see that, and he would prove it. So they had given up, though Alex kept suggesting they hire an inquiry agent. It was one of the things she was going to talk to him about in the city, while Julius kept his tryst with the Frenchwoman. Alex burned with the injustice of it all. He burned, too, with the terrifying notion that Julius had at last cracked his carapace of reality.

'A little cold,' Julius said as he drew near to Roxane. 'I hope it will be warmer in the city.' His hands were very white, Roxane noticed all at once. White and frail. A leap of that vulnerable love that is so close to pity shook her. 'Julius …' She hesitated to say any more, but now he was looking at her, inquiringly, eyebrows raised. 'You don't need to be so brave, you know. No-one's going to thank you for it.'

She had forgotten how forbidding he could look, and for a moment wondered if she was completely wrong, if she should just have forgotten he existed altogether. 'Brave? There is no bravery in truth. I know this is real. And I will prove it. I do not care how long it takes.'

'But Julius, you know that Pym—'

'Pym. Who is Pym? He does not exist. What exists is this sonata, this magnificent thing.' He said it as if despair had never touched his heart, as if the first few terrible weeks—months—after the revelation of Pym's hoax had not existed at all. Sandrine Delage, in the space of a few weeks, had succeeded in convincing him of the rightness of her claim. Roxane knew she should be grateful; Julius looked as if he were coming alive again, he was no longer the husk of his old self but emerging cautiously into a new skin—no longer successful biographer but the seeker after truth, no matter what it cost.

Roxane shivered and Julius said, 'Come, you are cold. Let's go.' He opened his door and stepped back into the car delicately, not concerning himself with her at all.

He had not questioned her motives for coming back, she thought as she opened her own door. He had never once asked her. He had just accepted. That was Julius' way. In the old days that had chilled and angered her, for it seemed like indifference. Later, she had thought that perhaps it was true subtlety, true understanding. Now, she didn't know anymore. It was just the way he was. She wasn't a novelist, like Alex, to wonder at the reaches of the heart. She felt her way along her own; how could she truly say she knew others'?

She knew that Isabelle and Alex found that sort of attitude unbelievable. They were of the same generation as Seth; a little older, but of the same cast. The generation that believed you could understand, if you talked long enough. If you were sincere enough. Like the people on the talk-back shows, and the people displaying their emotional wares on midday television. Anything could be understood, forgiven, dealt with, labelled nicely, filed away. As long as you were honest, even the most horrendous, the most sordid, the most inexplicable could be ironed out. She could just imagine Pym in such a show: he would explain earnestly, as he had done in the articles that had followed his great revelation. And it wouldn't matter if the explanation involved trampling on others, if it showed a heart white and cold and withered. That would be all the more interesting, all the more worthy of ten minutes in the voracious maw of TV. What happened afterwards, of course, to lives once caught in its grip was of no consequence.

Perhaps it was unfair of her to blame it on Seth's, on Alex's generation. After all, it was merely a logical extension of the growing hunger of the media for more, more and more chewed-up, spat-out fragments, more stories set to theme music. She remembered the TV show *Behind the Headlines*, the show Julius had refused to appear on, and which she could not bring herself to watch. Alex had, though, and he had said it had been soft, quiet, reverent, but full of a suppressed, vicious laughter. Pym had been utterly Pym, he had said to Roxane, that's the only way you can explain it. But since then Pym had dropped out of sight; he had not given anymore interviews. People had lost interest, she thought, but he was probably in there, badgering. But his fragment had been spat out. He was no longer news.

But then, neither was Julius. Even more so. Julius was worse than yesterday's news: he was the embarrassment of yesterday. All those people who had once been so reverent, so in awe of him—either they savaged him now, or worse, ignored him. They had always suspected, they would say. They had always felt something was not quite right. Only one person had thought to support Julius, apart from the family and Zauber's private gesture, and that was Sandrine Delage, assistant to Simonin, with little power to change anything, as Julius had said, with a strange kind of laughter.

Hearing him saying this, Roxane had felt her breath twisting in her chest. Of course, he had written back to the woman, the grand old man dispensing munificence even in his hour of need, and then he was lost. Why had she never seen that his seeming imperturbability concealed such a desire for approval? Even when he was reduced to the approval of the Madame Delages of this world. Then she had seen the interview with Mathilde Baudel, and her estimation of the woman had risen. It had been a surprisingly coherent and clever piece, and Julius had responded much more naturally to it than to her initial approach. Since then the two had corresponded fairly frequently, and Roxane knew that Julius looked forward to the letters, though he would never have admitted it. And now he was to meet her. For a moment Roxane thought of turning the car around, heading straight back home. It would be a kindness to Julius. But of course she did not, though afterwards she wondered what would have happened if she had given in to her instinct.

★

Cher Monsieur Newton,

You will be pleased to know that I have made more inquiries concerning Madame Augustine Bernard, late of France, who sailed to Australia with her soldier husband after the war. She was born near Bayonne to a well-off family around 1919 and was known to have had high musical abilities from a young age. Her family did indeed know Monsieur Ravel: her father belonged to an orchestra in Biarritz which had played some of his works, and they first met the maestro through business. I have found a small memoir written by the good lady which was deposited with the archives at Bayonne, and herewith enclose a copy.

I look forward to seeing you on Sunday 5th, at 10.30 a.m., as arranged. It will be a great privilege!

Most respectful good wishes,
Sandrine Delage (Madame)

DOCUMENT NO. 111067, 16 May, 1943, donated by BERNARD Augustine Marianne, subject: RAVEL Maurice

My name is Augustine Marianne Bernard, and I was born in Bayonne just after the Great War. My purpose in writing this small piece is to remember a few things from my childhood which may be of interest to future musical historians.

I lived a very privileged life. This is not to say that we lived in luxury, though we lived in comfort, certainly. No, the privilege lay in having known some of the most wonderful musicians and composers this earth has ever seen. My father, Monsieur Bernard, was well known, as he was not only in a popular orchestra, but also wrote columns on music for national publications. In that time before the present war, when the Pays Basque was a fashionable area for holidays, the most interesting people came to us. I met many people whose names are now legend to us; but the one whom I remember best of all, because his relationship with my family became greater than that of business, is Monsieur Maurice Ravel. Maurice Joseph Ravel, the great composer.

If I could only make you see him as I saw him then! He was a small man, but so well-kept, so carefully, beautifully thought out. He was so tender with us children, too; kind without any condescension, understanding our games, unlike most of the other adults around us. We went twice or three times to receptions at his apartment in Saint-Jean and, even there, in the midst of his beautiful things, his shining life, he was always there for us. He never said, No, don't touch, or frowned at us. He did not make light of us, like so many others did. He understood. There have been some who have said later that he was a strange man, given to weird and even unsavoury compulsions. I reject this absolutely. Monsieur Ravel was transparent as glass; and yet deep as the sea. He was a man of great reserve, but capable of great affection too.

Oh, I still remember the day of my birthday, when he came to see me in the shop, and he handed me a parcel, saying, 'This is for you, Augustine,' and then he stood there, smiling, while I opened it. It was, like all his presents, a beautiful thing, perfect, unlike anything I had ever seen before. A mermaid, under glass ...

Not long after, my poor Monsieur Ravel contracted that terrible illness, ataxia, I think it was called, which was eventually to take him away from us. I believe it first manifested itself in him after a minor car accident which had caused him to hit his head. However, his father had also died from some kind of brain illness, I believe—he was subject to terrible headaches. Be that as it may, our poor Monsieur Ravel did not come to my father's house anymore, but occasionally my father went to see him. We children could not go, because of Monsieur Ravel's sadly diminished state. I remember one day my father coming home late from such a trip, preoccupied and very sad. When we asked what was the matter, he shook his head and said he could not talk about it, that Monsieur Ravel was staring into the abyss, and that he, my father, had been privileged enough to do something very important for him. We did not question him further, for he seemed very agitated, and very sad. It made us sad, too, to think of the terrible things Fate had reserved for that most sweet man.

I write these things down so that they may be not lost, in these grim days of war: for who knows what will happen to us all afterwards?

To Geoffrey Zauber
Editor, *The Lyre*

Dear Geoffrey,
          I know you will be surprised to hear from me, but I would like you to read the enclosed—without prejudice!—and then to meet me and Madame Sandrine Delage in the foyer of the Hotel Figaro at 10. 30 a.m. on Sunday 5th. You were one of the few to write personally to me after the event of which we both know only too much, and I would like you to be one of the first to read of what has since transpired. Please, just let me know if you have received the material. Do not comment on it until after our meeting.

Yours,
Julius Newton
Encl: copies of interviews, document, letter

★

Dear Julius,
          Message received, and material. I'll be there. But—for God's sake, Julius, why weren't these things found before? You realise of course we must check them over and over. But even so, it does not prove Ravel wrote the sonata. Did your Madame Bernard write any more than this? I know what you're getting at, that perhaps this man Bernard wrote the sonata down for Ravel. But there is no proof of that. Still, I must admit it does make me feel excited—if uneasy.

I will keep any further comments till we meet. I am looking forward to that.

Sincerely,
Geoffrey

three

Thomas Albert Rice had never been one to look back gloatingly on past glories, but he would have been dishonest if, on the other hand, he had ignored them. He'd pulled off quite a few good stories in his day, and now that he'd reached that dangerous age when journalists decide they want the solidity of book covers, he wanted to see them well tied up. He had recently been offered a very attractive contract to write his book, the book he'd always meant to write. He even had a name picked out for it—*The First Casualty*. Came from some quote or other, about truth and war. Well, nearly all his important stories had been to do with the nature of truth.

He'd been writing the book for quite a while, reconstructing each case from the copious notes he'd kept, the articles, the tapes and transcripts. Other journalists he'd worked with had pages filled with ideas for novels, often based on life in newspaper offices, but

Rice wasn't interested in fiction. Truth, as he knew, was stranger than fiction. People were more interested in the truth, in real-life dramas, than in the dizzy and often clumsy constructions of the would-be novelists. And besides, he reckoned novels should be left to the novelists. They did not have the same kind of nature or imagination as journalists, although in a way both were detectives. Detectives of the human mind. No, his book would be a recollection in tranquillity of his own detection, his own case stories, his own depictions of human nature.

He knew the publishers were eager to get his manuscript, and he'd been working on it for months. Now he was at last working on what was a minor centrepiece of the book: the Ravel Sonata Affair. A minor centrepiece, because, of course, the major one was the Rossi murder, committed many years before. But even though the Ravel Sonata Affair was more of an exotic, odd little subject, it was nevertheless fascinating. He had immediately thought so when Pym had contacted him. Here was something that appealed to his sense of the bizarre.

It was while he was writing up the notes that he came on something Pym had said to him, all those months ago. Something about leaving clues to follow. Something caught his attention again. He reread his transcript: '... and all those clues I had scattered! Newton had studied Ravel for months, years; he knew that Poe was one of his favourite authors. Why, then, didn't he see?' At the time, he hadn't noticed it particularly, although of course he knew that part of the so-called letter had been lifted directly from that story of Poe's, but now it nagged at him. What had Poe to do with any of this?

It was then that he purchased a copy of the works of Poe, and begun reading. The man bored him: he remembered reading Poe at school and being fascinated, then quickly satiated. Poe was just too much. There was too much portentousness, though God knew the man delivered too: he could be as gory as Stephen King. But there was a wildness about the writing which made it curiously elusive, and curiously embarrassing after a while—it was as if the author was jumping up and down on tip-toe, calling out loudly to attract attention. And so he skipped through a whole lot of the stories—all the horror, the detection, the mystifications—until he arrived at the story that Pym had mentioned, the story that made the hairs prickle on the back of Rice's neck.

The Narrative of Arthur Gordon Pym. It was a hoax story of Poe's, purportedly collected by him from a young man called Arthur Gordon Pym; an odd account of several disordered voyages to strange places, ending in an enigmatic trip to a polar region where Pym and his companions' boat simply drifted into an all-encompassing whiteness. The story was postscripted with a note from Poe, the 'editor', drawing attention to Pym's unfortunate death in a later accident. And then, the strange inscription supposedly seen by Pym on rocks at an island he had visited, and Poe's 'translation': *I have graven it within the hills, and my vengeance upon the dust of the rock.*

Like many of Poe's stories this one carried strange baggage indeed. One of the episodes in it concerned three men, including Pym, and a cabin boy, Richard Parker, floating on the ocean after a shipwreck, getting hungrier and more desperate, till at last Parker proposed that one of them should be eaten to save the others. But it was he who drew the short straw. Fifty years after Poe's story was published, three survivors of a shipwreck were rescued after spending several days at sea. It soon became apparent that there had once been a fourth survivor, a cabin boy called Richard Parker …

Rice read with a mounting excitement. He was not one to be affected by such horror stories, of course, but aware of their potential. He could see his story taking shape, and all the superlatives he would use. He had tried to contact Julius Newton, but had been told first by the dragon of a sister that he was speaking to no-one, then that he was out, then, yesterday, he had got somebody or other who told him that 'Dr and Miss Newton have gone to the city for an indefinite period'.

And that had only confirmed the vague uneasiness that had been building in him. For he had tried to contact Pym many times over the last few weeks, and had not been able to trace him at all. The landlady of the boarding house where he had stayed previously said that he had left months ago, and no, she did not know where he had gone. He had tried all kinds of leads, but it was no use. Pym had utterly vanished— disappeared into thin air, not unlike his namesake in Poe's story. So, two weeks or so ago, after much debate with himself, he had filed a missing persons notification at the police station, and also inserted notices in the newspapers. He held little hope that either action would lead to Pym, but you never knew. Meanwhile, he would keep working on the rest of his notes. And he would try and track down Newton, too, at his nephew's place, for he imagined that was where he would be staying.

He was convinced now that Newton knew much more than he had ever said; but if he had, if he had known the sonata to be a fraud, why on earth had he allowed Pym to expose him? The sort of person Newton was—a grand old man of letters—that sort of person never allowed himself to be used in that way. Unless he had no choice. None of it made any sense, on the face of it, and Tom Rice was determined to uncover the truth.

They arrived at Alex's house earlier than they had expected. Julius, despite the long drive, insisted on taking a train into the city immediately on some mysterious errand of his own, and refused to allow anyone to accompany him. So Roxane, glad anyway not to have to cope with his delusions, stayed at home with Alex and Isabelle, watching them as they went about their family life, and noting how Alex acted quite differently here, on his home turf. Watching them, she'd been aware of some slight regret, or maybe, if she was honest, deep regret, about what they shared. She and Seth's father, Martin, had never had anything like that. And not for the first time she felt respect for Alex, for what he had so painfully carved out for himself from the ruins of a difficult childhood.

'It's good to see you,' she had said, trying to imbue the words with meaning. She still could not quite say what she meant. Perhaps I was wrong to decry the younger generation's loquaciousness, she thought, perhaps sometimes words can have an effect, can be real, life-changing things. But for her and Martin, it was much too late. Much much too late. And for poor Julius too ... .

'It's good to see you too, Roxane,' Alex said, smiling. There was something changed in him, something more solid, she thought suddenly. Not fixed; just less wavery, somehow.

Then Isabelle had declared she needed an hour or so, while the twins were in bed, to put the finishing touches to an illustration she was doing for a book cover, and she'd suggested Alex and Roxane go out for a walk. The look she gave her husband as she said this, the look of tender complicity, of relaxed knowledge, gripped at Roxane's heart.

Outside was crisp and dry, the sky pale with early autumn. Because it was the middle of the day, the suburb was fairly quiet; there was the odd swish of a car on the streets, the odd hammering going on somewhere. Children were at school, adults at work or else in their homes, having light lunches and listening to midday radio or watching TV. Each house in its neat or not-so-neat yard; each gate firmly or carelessly closed; each streetside window demurely veiled. Behind the gates, behind the doors, in each little capsule of light and space, whole lives went on, unobserved, so that dreadful tragedies or unbelievable comedies could be acted out without anyone else knowing. Alex thought of the old cities he'd lived in in Europe; thought of the chairs out on doorsteps, the called-out comments, the faces hanging out of windows, gossiping. But even in Europe there were places like this: Isabelle had told him of her grandmother's grand apartment block, where each tenant lived in perfect bourgeois privacy. Still, even there, people going out to walk their dogs or do the shopping would stop and talk, would pass the time of day with the concierge. Whereas here ... he didn't even know the neighbours on their left, though the right-hand neighbours were very nice. It was an odd feeling, the intimacy of a street—all the houses close together, but without any intimacy at all really. Like being in a lift with strangers: you tried to make the space around you inviolable.

He said as much to Roxane, who smiled. 'I used to want to know the neighbours too,' she said. 'Now though, I'm not so keen. And you know, Alex, those people in Europe whom you admire so much, that might not be real intimacy at all. It might simply be plain old gossip.'

'There's nothing plain about gossip! That's how we work out what we think of life, of people's behaviour, of each other. And after all, what is a novel, for instance, but gossip? Chat about other people? Feelings like there-but-for-the-grace-of-God, or feelings of revulsion, a working out of human nature: gossip does that, and books. Not only novels. What Julius writes, too.'

Roxane smiled at him. 'Yes Alex.' That was part of the change, she thought. The way he spoke about Julius. The way he spoke to Julius. There was something oddly disconcerting about it; some kind of half-serene tenderness that still masked anxiety.

Alex flushed a little. 'I didn't mean to be preachy,' he said, misinterpreting. 'I can't help myself. Isabelle says I should relax.'

Roxane squeezed his arm. 'Don't apologise.' They walked on in silence for a moment, then Alex said, 'Do you think … do you think Julius truly believes that the sonata is real? I mean, perhaps he might be going to write something …'

Roxane said, 'He wants to believe.' But was that true? Maybe that was what being close to someone meant. You could never quite believe either in their villainy or their heroism, their fame or their infamy.

'You know Julius the best,' Alex said. He looked rather sad. And that was what was so disconcerting. That his new feeling for Julius seemed genuine. And that Julius seemed to have understood it too. Without saying a word one way or the other, he had shifted gears so that now it seemed the most natural thing in the world for him to stay with Alex when he was in the city.

'I don't know if Julius will ever write again,' she said firmly. There was no real proof of that—there was no real reason why Julius shouldn't write another book. Except for shame. For fear of the comments of others. Had Hugh Trevor-Roper written more after the Hitler diaries fiasco? Had Max Harris continued after the Ern Malley affair? She wasn't sure, but she felt that perhaps the heart had gone out of them, despite their attempts to maintain dignity and a generous spirit. And Julius was old. Older than either of those men when it had happened to them; more vulnerable to the king-hit, precisely because his reputation was already so well-established. Something like this turned everyone into a revisionist. All his other work would now only be seen as unreliable anecdotes. She certainly knew that if it was her, she would have been unable to write another word. Of any kind.

'Julius told me that another publisher has taken on the rights to the other books,' Alex said.

'Yes.' Roxane looked at her nephew, and he laid his hand momentarily on her arm. I don't deserve this look, this tenderness, she thought, near tears. But her voice was light and dry as she went on, 'Julius believes things will work out.'

'And you don't.'

'I can't see—well, I am a terrible pessimist, and I believe that once something like this happens, things can never work out completely.'

'People forget,' Alex said. 'They change their minds too.' He stopped and looked at her, his eyes open, guileless, and she remembered how he'd looked like that, long ago, and the past had her by the throat again. Maybe he hadn't changed at all—he'd always been like this, and she had simply put him aside, because her life then had been so painful.

'Don't they?' he added.

Roxane managed to smile. She could hardly begin, now, to respond to him warmly when their relationship had always been so careful, so delicate, so bound up with the individual's right to the privacy of emotion. It would bewilder him, frighten him.

'The Delage woman has persuaded Julius of what he wants to believe. Now, people might very well forget or change their minds, but to what extent? I'm not sure at all.'

'But why not? After all, Julius' story might be true.'

'Alex.' Roxane stopped and faced him. 'You know the tests were done on the photo and the letter, and it was absolutely proven they'd been concocted. But very cleverly. Pym was a musician. It was not difficult for him to forge the sonata as well.'

'But Julius says that's impossible. He says you can't forge the spirit—'

'That's not the opinion I've heard. Anyway, I think he should forget it. Whether it's genuine or not, no-one's going to believe him now.'

'I would like to find that Pym,' Alex said. 'I would like to ask why, *why*? It's crazy.'

'You and me both.'

They walked in silence for a while, then Alex said, 'There's an inquiry agent I know of. Perhaps we could think of … After all, there are some clues. That letter, for instance. Why pick on that Poe story? We could find out if …'

'No, Alex.'

'We don't have to tell Julius. Look, Roxane, I think we have to do more than just let this guy get away with it. I want to know. I want it explained.' He stopped and looked at her, his eyes bright with emotion.

Roxane looked coolly at her nephew. 'Sometimes there is no explanation, Alex. After all, it's Julius' life. Not yours.'

Alex flushed again. 'Okay, Okay, I know what you're driving at. But I want this for Julius, not to satisfy my curiosity. His life's been destroyed. By the meaningless malevolence of some candied creature.'

'Oh, lovely description.' Roxane smiled. 'But you know, Alex, your uncle is not quite the victim you seem to have decided he is. He is … oh …'

There he was, always anxious yet self-important, chivvying them. 'Alexander! Roxane!' And the pair of them, the twins, giggling, playing tricks on him, not realising how insecure he was and yet perhaps in some subterranean way quite aware of it, with the innocent amorality of children. Alexander once whispered to her, 'Julius was born old,' and she'd laughed, and nodded, and said, 'With slippers on his feet!' Julius had heard. But he'd only got more bossy, more anxious.

'Alexander! Roxane!' He never called her or her brother by a shortened version. They called him Jules behind his back, but never up front. 'Come and see this.' He took it upon himself to show them the world. But being Julius, it was never just wonder, never just surprise at the marvels, the grossness, the strangeness. It was an opportunity to lecture. 'See here, this ladybird, it has more spots than usual …' And off he'd go, talking, and then look at them, grave and satisfied. More often than not they did not dare laugh at him. They remembered their father, his hectoring tone to poor Julius; the way he doted on them, the love-children of his old age. Who knew what kind of indignities Julius had had to suffer? When they first became aware of him, he was already so much older. Anxious eyes, thin legs. Trying to keep away from their father.

Alex cleared his throat. 'Perhaps ... you know my idea, Roxane, of writing Julius' biography. No, don't look at me like that. I still think it would be a good idea. And it would show other people the real person, not this ... this figment of the imagination that's been created. And perhaps ...' He looked quickly at her. 'Perhaps you could write some things down too, Roxane. About your childhood with him, that sort of thing. You know. Maybe it could help. Not with Pym, maybe, but with... with other things.' His voice, which had risen almost to a squeak, only just reached her, and she pulled herself back with an effort. He was looking at her with what she now knew was love, and pity, and she was aware of it. From the centre of his warm family, the life he'd created for himself behind one of those brick walls he so decried, he no doubt saw her life, and that of her brother, as incomplete. And maybe they were. But Roxane no longer knew what completion meant. It could have so many different meanings, at different ages.

'I can't write. I'm not a writer. My words are too controlled. They mean nothing.' But there was something inside her saying yes, yes. I cannot hold this inside me anymore. I cannot.

'Roxane.' He touched her lightly again. He didn't speak. But for once that silence was not the usual Newton minefield, full of evasion. It was a moment that made her feel just a little stronger, just a little more ready to keep going, and deep inside her an astonishment grew at the transformation, the emerging of her nephew from his lifelong chrysalis.

four

TAPE 1, Roxane Newton

The other day, I was given a challenge. I cannot write my story, for if I see the words there, I'll take fright. I was never good with words, unlike Julius. I always felt like I couldn't touch them, that they had more power than I was willing to go near. But a tape like this, I can simply wipe it all, so perhaps it is a good idea. Sort out things myself, in the ether, in the space of this recording. Talking to myself. That's supposed to be important, isn't it? To sort things out. It's what we're meant to do, we modern humans. Oh look, there I go, just can't resist. You never know, it may help, somehow, though I doubt it.

To start from the beginning ... I was born in the dog years of the war, in a leafy suburb that hasn't changed a great deal since then. My mother had been a writer of sorts as a young woman, but I believe she easily gave it up for marriage, once she met my father. When I first was aware of him, my father was an ex-military man, the stress being on the ex. It was a situation he felt keenly, and visited daily on my mother, and my oldest brother Julius, but not on us, the twins, the children of his old age. I say old, but now, you know, Julius is older than Father was then. As a child, I was not at all afraid of my father, though I knew Julius slunk around near him. But Alexander and I, we could do no wrong. He would have liked it, I think, if my mother and Julius could have disappeared, so he would have us to himself—except for the fact that he didn't much like having anything to do with the logistical elements of looking after children. Father went to the office every day during the war, and he had to put up with the indignity of seeing the son he so despised both go to war and distinguish himself there as well. It seems a rather cruel justice that the daughter who was the apple of his eye barely remembers anything about him, while the son who went in daily fear of him has shaped his life around a rejection of everything he stood for.

When I was about seven, my father died. Julius was twenty-two by this stage, he was already quite grown-up—mind you, I can't remember a time when he wasn't. I can't imagine him as a sulky adolescent at all! Mother did not try to force him to look after us—it was he who decided, quite by choice, to come home. He had joined up in 1942, and had been sent to Europe along with some others. He was at the liberation of Paris in 1944; from that time he acquired his knowledge of French language and culture, something which has stayed with him all his life. Before the war, though, he'd got preferential placement in a university course, and was doing brilliantly. But he stopped that, once he came back home. He got a job writing pieces for travel brochures and pamphlets, but I can still remember seeing him, at night, his head bent over papers, studying everything he could find about music; not its technical aspects, but rather the psychologies of musicians and composers. He'd always been fond of music, you see. Father also had liked music, up to a point; but he affected to hate all German music, and also, for a while, French composers. He said the Germans were tainted; and as for the French, they were too soft and frivolous. Julius had never said anything to these stupidities, but like my mother, he was stubborn in the way quiet, seemingly weak people often are. Anyway, at this time Julius started on the works which were to bring him such fame—listening to records on his new record-player, annotating, coming home with piles of books, discussing endlessly with Mother, who blossomed like a rose under the sun of her Julius' regard.

We were only young children, Alexander and I. Yet we knew that for our mother, we were tainted by our father's regard. Oh, she looked after us well, she dealt fairly and kindly with us. But did she love us? I'm not sure; though I'm inclined to believe she thought she did. I can still hear her saying, 'Honestly, Roxane, don't be so ridiculous!' But Alexander, your father, and I, we weren't unhappy. Don't get that idea. We were secure, at peace, in a house that hummed with purpose and tranquillity. I think we half-forgot our father, and took to seeing Julius as he. There was nothing strange about that, though I can imagine the sly insinuations people would make these days when everything has to be 'explained' by sexual abuse or what have you. There's altogether too much suggestiveness in our times, I think. There was nothing funny going on between my mother and Julius; they were simply content. In that situation, perhaps, they could be their true selves. Mother as matriarch, serenely undisturbed by a man's rankness; Julius as the eternal uncle—kind, obliging, always a little anxious.

I don't remember him ever bringing women home, or men either come to that. I think he is one of those rare souls for whom sex holds no interest. Which is not to say that he didn't understand it; on the contrary, his depictions of Beethoven in love, for instance, are so vivid that you almost feel as if he's in his skin. And there was something more to that portrayal too, something terrifying. Beethoven is portrayed, gleefully almost, as ... well, not to put too fine a point on it, as a pyschopath. I can remember a quote from the book that stuck in my head for ages: 'For Beethoven, love was not a healing, or a mirror of self: it was a consuming. A consuming of himself, and of the loved one. The music was a cannibal's feast ...'

I think that's what made the book so memorable for people, even the very few who hated it, who panned the book ferociously, who said it was vacuous, silly in its easy shock: here was Julius saying something that had never been said before. I reread the book recently and was struck, actually, by how dated it seemed, and I remembered then what those critics had said. But at the time, you must realise, it broke new ground. His later books were different, much calmer, although elegant and always popular. Anyway, I'm jumping ahead of myself.

Life was quite uneventful for us as children, except for the adventures we concocted ourselves. It was during that time, while we were going to school, getting grazed knees, setting up jokes and tricks together, that Julius began to build up his reputation. He published his first book, the Beethoven book, which, as you know, has gone into several reprints, and started work on his second. He was always a very meticulous writer, spending months over one small question. He also began to be asked to contribute to radio and TV programmes, to write magazine columns, and so forth. He also had lots of friends—even before any of the books were published, there were always people calling for him at our house.

I can remember sitting there, as a child, listening to all this conversation about music, amazed that anyone could talk so much. I think he'd made lots of contacts and acquaintances when he was in France too, at the end of the war, and it was amazing to me to see all these exotic people talking English in unusual accents, smoking Gauloises and so on. Alexander and I used to imitate their voices sometimes, it was really funny. We'd sit in a corner, holding our sides, repeating and giggling. Mother found us one day, and it was the first time I'd seen her really angry. She hauled us out by our arms really roughly, and made us apologise to the middle-aged Frenchwoman and her young male companion who were there that day—I think during the time Julius was working on the Beethoven book. I think she was a pianist or some kind of musician, and the young man was her relative, or student or whatever—things that didn't cut much ice with us, I'm afraid. I remember the woman smiling and saying, 'They are only children, madame,' but I did not appreciate that much. I realised she was trying to be kind, but because I hadn't been, it just made me feel angry. And guilty too, because the young man with her had flushed bright red at the interruption; he'd been talking earnestly with Julius, and we had broken into his talk, I suppose.

He was one of those painfully thin, painfully shy-looking people who can make your skin crawl with the flayed look of them. But then, of course, I just felt cranky. Silly old frog, I said to myself, ignoring my mother, who took us off outside, saying didn't we know how to be well-mannered, and what would these people think of our brother, and we should show them our best side, and so on. But they haven't come to see us, I thought angrily. Just him. Julius.

As time passed, he became more and more famous. Mother glowed in his glory, and Alexander and I, well, we just got on with our lives. At the age of twenty, Alexander met the love of his life, Sarah, your mother. This did not please Julius. He did not approve of people marrying young; in fact, I think he thought of marriage, or any close relationship between man and woman, as something that interfered too much. He'd had a life mapped out for Alexander, and for me, we soon came to realise. And those lives did not include early marriage. He did all he could, in his quiet, tenacious way, to stop your parents from marrying. Alexander even told me that Julius had gone to see Sarah's parents and painted a disconcerting picture of his own brother. That's what Alexander said, but by that stage he wasn't necessarily rational about Julius. What I certainly know is that he tried to enlist my support, playing on my undoubted geminal resentment of Sarah, but I knew that if I joined in that campaign, I would lose Alexander. It was selfish of me, purely selfish. Now I think of my brother and his wife, forever surrounded with the golden glow of their love, their understanding of each other, and the picture is both a joy and a terrible grief. Anyway, after that Alexander and Julius were estranged for quite a while. Alexander was one of those people who always like to think well of others, but his generosity failed him a little when it came to Julius. It was Sarah who reconciled them, finally—she wanted everyone to be as happy as she was, I think— but there was always a wariness afterwards.

Me, I stayed with Julius and Mother in our house. When Mother died, I still stayed on.

And then I decided to go back to university. It was something I'd always promised myself. You see, I'd had a quick training as a teacher, after I left school, but I wanted more. I was thirsty, hungry, starving for knowledge. Julius approved, but found it slightly amusing. He said I'd soon discover what a hotbed of mediocrity university was. I still think part of that was due to the fact he'd never finished his own course. He often decried academics, though I think his manner of working is extremely academic, and he was certainly happy enough to be invited to universities to give talks and such, and at one stage had his own honorary position at one university. He was that rare figure, a good media performer, an intelligent writer, but analytical and careful enough to find favour with the academy. I was amazed by my brother, I can tell you. I still am.

I suppose when you have someone like that in your family, it's hard to escape some pique. Of course, I went through the usual thing—why is he being listened to, when I'm not? What is it about his manner that leads him to have such a charmed life? And yet, there was no way Alexander or I could ever hate our brother, even later, when he'd behaved so badly towards both of us. There is something ... something vulnerable about Julius, though outsiders don't usually see it. Most of the time, I was glad for him; I liked reading his books, always have, for they're usually such a pleasure, well written, perfectly put together. Except for the Beethoven book, which was an odd mixture really. But a book you couldn't ignore. Sometimes too, I come across things which disconcert me utterly, things which make me think that maybe I don't know my brother at all. Then I think, How does a person who has such insight into another's mind get to be so clumsy in his personal relations?

Anyway, I digress. I was up to when I went to uni. It was in the sixties, an exciting time, I suppose, to be there. Except I was older than the average student. I was in my late twenties, had already had a job. But in some ways I was younger than them. Oh sure, I had already had a lover, and I remember it distressing Julius when I said that: he thought it was vulgar, I think. But the kids who were in my classes at uni seemed to have no holds on them—they said the most incredible things, and that made them seem glamorous indeed. I must say now that there was a lot of talk going on in those days, but I was too dazzled to realise that a lot of it was just talk.

Some of the lecturers were like that too—regular King Arthurs, with their strange, new Round Tables clustered about them. There was one fellow, Martin Cosgrove, in his late thirties, a lecturer in the English department; he was very well known on campus. I'd never met anyone like him before, but then, as Julius would say, I'd had a sheltered life. He was an amazingly good lecturer, we thought, who really loved and knew his stuff; his papers were brilliant, his opinions sought after. Now, I wonder if I reread those lectures of his, what would I feel? I fear I would find them dated too. Martin was someone who thrived on hero-worship, not only the open-mouthed worship of the younger students, but the more tempered admiration of the so-called mature age students, like me. But I didn't feel very mature, faced with Martin; I'd had sexual contact with a couple of men before that, but never had I really experienced what you might call love. Martin changed all that.

Martin knew of my feelings from a long way back, but he held his distance for quite a while. He often singled me out at tutorials, asking my advice, my ideas, on various things, in a way I both loved and hated. Loved, because it implied I was his equal; hated, because it singled me out as the oldest in the group. It was known that Martin was married, though none of the kids had seen his wife; but it was also well known that he had a kind of *droit de seigneur* as well as far as female students were concerned. It was the sort of time when such things were both expected and feared; we wanted to push beyond respectable boundaries but did not see that often such things were merely old habits in a new guise. The sexual revolution extended as far as women being deemed available to men; the other way round was more problematical!

However, there I was, chagrined yet relieved that Martin obviously did not see me as a possible bed-partner. It meant more quietness but also disappointment. It meant I was free to indulge in fantasies about him, without having to contend with the disagreeable truth of his shallowness. For we had all seen it—a girl aglow with the delight of being chosen as his Guinevere, only to eventually slink into tutorials red-eyed, trying hard to be revolutionarily brave and not to cling. It was well known Martin hated clinging.

I'd been speaking to Julius about Martin, and to Martin about Julius, for some time. It was one of those things I'd casually let drop into conversation, that my brother was the famous Julius Newton. Although now I wonder if Martin didn't know all along, if, in fact, he had focused on me because I was Julius' sister. I knew it was a good move, for Martin was fascinated with anything pertaining to fame. Julius, however, had been more circumspect. I thought rather resentfully that only Julius was of true interest to Julius.

One day, after a particularly stimulating tutorial, I went up to Martin and invited him to dinner the following weekend. He raised a quizzical eyebrow, so that I found myself blushing, and hurriedly said it would be at Julius' house, and that Julius would love to meet him, and so forth. He smiled then, and said he'd be more than happy to come. Then I said that his wife, of course, would be welcome too, but he just shook his head gently, and said she didn't much like going out. I nodded stupidly, hardly listening, imagining the great Martin Cosgrove in our house, sitting at our table, making conversation with Julius, and telling myself at the same time that I was an idiot, that I was far too old to be indulging in this kind of empty-headed nonsense. It doesn't always seem to help, knowledge of yourself, despite what the psychotherapy school tells you. You can recognise your own stupidities yet still repeat them. Have they thought of that?

Julius, of course, had boned up thoroughly on Martin's subject and delicately steered the conversation in and out of its harbours and shallows. Martin had made no such effort with Julius' interests, though he did at least know the names of his books. He told Julius that he never listened to classical music, that it was the music of the oppressor, and that as far as he was concerned only traditional music held any interest. Julius listened courteously but I knew what his views were; I had been subjected to enough of them in the past. To some extent, I agreed with both of them. I loved classical music, but did not see why that should divorce me from other kinds—from jazz, from folk and traditional music, even rock. But I said nothing.

Fortunately, my other brother and his family were also there—it was a few months before Alexander's and Sarah's deaths—so I did not have to enter into any damaging revelations. You were there too, Alex, that evening; you were only about six or maybe seven then, a sweet, but rather demanding little boy who had insisted on having dinner with us. Martin had said, when he came in and met you, 'Ah, yes, that age, it's not too easy,' in the kind of way that made me realise he must have a child too. I saw Alexander take this in too; saw his surprise that Martin should have come alone. Alexander was perfectly devoted as a husband and father, and I don't mean that in any derogatory sense at all. He had found his vocation; he was perfectly happy.

During dinner, you became too sleepy to stay at the table and were carried off to bed by your father. You were a forceful yet tender child, filled with the kind of force that comes from knowing that you are loved. Poor little boy! You used to annoy Julius sometimes, perhaps because of this very characteristic, something Julius had never been able to feel for himself. But he was kind enough; he was certainly kind enough after you were orphaned ... kind, but without the instinctive knowledge a child needs. Kind, but blank. And I ... well, I was too preoccupied. I didn't know. I suppose in some ways I thought that you must be alright. You had a home, plenty of food, all the material things you wanted. Now it chills me to the marrow, thinking of it. I may not have had satisfactory parents—who has? But at least I had them. You had only pictures in your head ... only ghosts to measure up to. No rebellion, no fighting for identity. Just ... kindness.

That evening ... that was the first time Martin ... I felt Martin's hand on my knee. At first, I thought it was a mistake, that someone had brushed against me without meaning to. Then I felt it again, quite firmly. My heart fluttered, as much in panic as anything else. I could see Martin's eyes on me; they were full of unmistakeable meaning. I kept talking, feeling my cheeks heating up, hearing my own voice going on heedlessly. Sarah was looking at me in some surprise, but Julius appeared not to have noticed anything. And Martin was, if anything, even more relaxed. Besides that one look, he did not give me any other visual clues to his feelings—except for that bold hand insinuating itself, getting bolder, more difficult to ignore. At last, I stumbled up, muttering something about getting coffee, and Sarah followed me, while the three men sat there quite at ease, still chattering.

There was something both exciting and shaming about what had happened. I felt as if I were years younger; horribly unsure, yet horribly confident too. For once, I was glad of the still rigid sex roles that insisted women make the coffee. Sarah looked at me curiously as I boiled water and arranged coffee cups. 'Are you alright, Roxane?'

'Sure, sure ...' I said.

'I thought ...' she said, then hesitated. Our family have never been great at confidences. Sarah came from a much more open family, but she had learnt that, apart from Alexander, we were shy about opening our hearts. So, instead, she began talking about you, and your exploits at school, but I could hardly hear what she was saying. The blood was pounding in my head, repeating over and over again, 'Martin wants me ... me ... me ...'

But he didn't do anything about it, not at that time anyway. He went home quite tamely, after thanking Julius for his hospitality—notice he didn't thank me! He just said he'd see me at uni on Monday, then was off, his plaits bouncing on his shoulders. When he had gone, Julius shook his head. 'The lengths young people go to nowadays,' he said gently. 'But he's not a bad fellow, intelligent, if a little ... er ...'

'I didn't like him much,' Alexander declared, looking at me. 'I don't trust him.' Julius looked at me sharply then, as if he'd only just realised what everyone else seemed to assume—that Martin was more than just my lecturer. I shrugged, not meeting his glance, feeling a sense of unease for no real reason.

On Monday I was back at uni, when Martin called me into his office. As I closed the door, my hands were slippery with sweat. I knew what he would do, what he would say. But he motioned me to a chair.

'Interesting dinner, the other night,' he said, his eyes full on me. I could barely bring myself to nod. 'A most interesting man, Julius.' He paused, and regarded the end of his pen. I suddenly thought, Oh God, he's too shy, he doesn't know how to go on; after all, I'm not one of his eighteen-year-olds, I'm not going to be consumed. What a fool! It pains me to think of it now.

He said, still looking at his pen, 'Roxane.' I thrilled at his saying my name; it acquired a kind of glamour in his mouth. I said stupidly, truculently, because I wasn't sure how else to react, 'Yes, what do you want?'

'You,' he said simply. He got up from his desk, and walked towards me, arms held out. I was in them before I'd even noticed; then he was murmuring, 'The door, let's lock it,' and I had time to think, Why? I don't care who sees me. But he soon stopped all of that kind of thing.

five

Whatever else Tom Rice was, he wasn't a man given to fancies. At least not fancies of the Poe sort, of all kinds of unspeakable crimes and strange horrors. But he had seen enough of the strangeness of the human heart to realise that truth came in many guises. And that you could not discount the outlandish or the bizarre, because to someone else they might make perfect sense. So the first time the unbidden, outlandish notion of what might have happened to Pym came into his head, he didn't reject it outright, but he didn't give it a lot of skull-space either. Still, when he had rung the police the other day and asked whether any progress had been made on his missing person notification, he wasn't surprised to have been told that there was little progress as yet. He did not mention the notion that had come into his head. In the course of his career, he had had occasion to observe the police at work, and knew not to underestimate them. But he was hopeful of being able to stitch up something rapidly for his book, something which would make the case an even more exciting centrepiece. His palms tingled with the premonition he always got when a story almost too hot to handle began its slow unravelling in front of him.

He pulled the telephone towards himself and began to dial. The phone rang and rang, and he drummed his fingers on the table. He crashed the receiver down, and dialled again. Finally, a click, then a recorded voice saying, 'We are sorry we cannot come to the phone right now, but if you …'

'No, I bloody well won't!' Rice slammed the phone down. It wasn't often that he gave in to his temper, but today it was an outlet for the restless excitement that had seized him. He drummed his fingers again, then, coming to a sudden decision, put on his jacket, shouldered his bag, and let himself out of the house.

Sandrine Delage was still jetlagged. She had never been on such a long plane journey. The fateful Indonesian journey Professeur Simonin had undertaken had not been his first to that part of the world, but Sandrine had never accompanied him. She stood in her room at the Hotel Figaro, looking out over a magnificent sweep of water—turquoise sequinned with platinum—and sighed with happiness. The fact that she was lightheaded with lack of sleep did not blot out the extraordinary sensation of the Australian light, so bright and clear even in the city that she wondered how it would be out in the country. She hoped she would have time to take a trip and see. Sandrine had always lived in the South of France, so sun itself was not a stranger to her, but this light was something she had not encountered. In the Pays Basque, it was still muted, still slightly veiled. She had heard somewhere that if Australia had been in the northern hemisphere, it would be on the same latitude as Morocco. But Morocco was a desert, wasn't it? This was clearly not a desert, she thought, with its canopy of trees whose leaves glittered so alluringly, but that allusion to Morocco was somehow not quite as outlandish as it might have seemed.

She stepped out onto the balcony. The city was well and truly awake, horns were blaring, people click-clacking just below her; a whole work day starting, yet to her it seemed slightly absurd to work in this sunshine, in those bright clothes that made everything seem like a holiday. She looked down at her own cream suit and simple shoes with some indecision. If le Docteur Newton was anything like these people she could see parading below, then she might look a little too formal. But no, she would feel wrong in a little dress. She had come for work, for important meetings. She did not want to feel like she was on holiday, just yet.

She reluctantly went back inside and opened her briefcase. The precious documents were in the middle, carefully protected. She opened them out again, merely for the pleasure of seeing them. The familiar skip of excitement began in her chest.

The phone rang shrilly. She jumped, and picked it up.

'Mrs Delage. There is a visitor for you downstairs. A Dr Julius Newton.'

He was sitting in one of the foyer's large armchairs, his back to her as she emerged from the lift. She had thus a small opportunity to observe him before he saw her. She could see a well-shaped head, still thickly covered with shining white hair. She could see a fragile frame under a dark jacket, and a certain cast to the body that gave the impression of something held in check. She thought briefly of what he had written: the books, the articles. He gave plenty of interviews but nowhere had he really given a clue as to the essential man. And then she was at his side, and they were exclaiming, and introducing themselves.

'I am a little early, I know. Perhaps we should have coffee?' He was still a nice-looking man, though there was a small tremble to his hands that she hadn't expected, an air of frailty. She was glad she had put on her cream suit; he was dressed in a careful, polished sort of way that suggested here was someone for whom the appropriate attire was important. He was looking at her with a gentle, rather attractive smile, and she found herself warmed by it.

'Why yes, that would be very nice.' Sandrine's English was very good, as she regularly went to England for work, but she was a little self-conscious about her accent, which her English friends had characterised as 'sweet'. She was too aware of the nuances of English to feel entirely comfortable with that description, but Dr Newton certainly made no comment. She had heard Australians were quite different. In a nation of immigrants, no accent was bound to attract too much attention, surely.

'I think perhaps the hotel coffee shop. It looks quite acceptable.' He certainly had an attractive manner, she thought. But then, she was old-fashioned, not able to deal, as her friends told her, with the directness of much of what passed for modern manners. She smiled. 'That will be fine then.'

They had still not said a word about what had brought them both here, but Sandrine thought Julius Newton was not the type of man to rush at anything. It would come, in time, after they had exhausted all the ritual feints, the gentle probings of intention on both sides. She had read a great deal about *l'Affaire Ravel*, as it was known in France, and knew that Julius was not necessarily always wise, or always made the right decisions. But she felt sure he had understood from the beginning that at the affair's centre, there was a kernel of truth. And that truth lay in the music. She had no idea why a person like Pym should seek to do what he had done; for her, all that mattered was the music, and its truth. The sonata was by Ravel; she felt it, knew it.

They sat at the uncomfortably low tables of the coffee lounge, drank excellent coffee and ate sticky, crisp Italian pastries. They spoke of France, of music, of Professeur Simonin. But not of Ravel, nor of the sonata. Little by little, she felt, they became more comfortable with each other, yet still reserved; he persisted in calling her madame, she addressed him as docteur.

It was only after all the coffee had been drunk, all the cakes disposed of, and all the polite preliminaries suitably dispensed, that Sandrine brought out her document case. 'You have seen many of these, of course, but ...'

She was surprised when he interrupted. 'Please excuse me. I have just seen ...' He was standing up, gesturing at someone on the other side of the roon. 'I hope you do not mind, but I have asked someone else to join us. The editor of *The Lyre*, Geoffrey Zauber.'

'Of course I do not mind.' But Sandrine was disappointed. She had been so looking forward to the time when she would show Docteur Newton the latest research, the interesting sidelights she was sure they could follow. She watched as Geoffrey Zauber approached. He was a very tall, very large man dressed in an untidy suit, with curly, greying hair rioting over his head. His smile was broad as he approached them.

'Julius. Good to see you.' Sandrine noticed that he grasped Julius' hand firmly, warmly, almost reassuringly. Then he turned to her. 'Madame Delage. A pleasure to meet you.'

'And I you.' She felt a little uncertain; her treasured scenario changing. But perhaps this was for the better.

'Well, it appears you have already indulged in a little coffee. Perhaps we could adjourn to the lounge and talk there?'

'Certainly. Why not.' Julius got up rather stiffly. 'We have a lot to talk about.' But he said this without enthusiasm, and Sandrine was surprised, and a little dismayed. But then of course one had to remember that Dr Newton had been through a very difficult period of his life, and he was clearly not over it yet.

At last, they were settled on the leather lounges; the soft-footed hotel life going on around them, the sun pouring in through the huge plateglass windows. The sun on the back of Sandrine's neck began to make her feel slow, less eager to get on with business. She listened as Geoffrey and Julius talked briefly of people she did not know, then smiled as they excused themselves for being so rude, and told them she hadn't minded at all.

Finally, Geoffrey said, 'Julius tells me you've got some very interesting information.'

Sandrine's papers were already out. She began speaking rapidly. 'Some Dr Newton has already seen, others are newer. There is also a short report on the manuscript paper of the title sheet which Dr Newton sent to us, and you will note that it says this type of manuscript paper was indeed in common use in the mid-1930s, as was the type of ink. But that is only a small thing. Please read carefully the biographical details on the Bernard family, as I believe they will be of great use to us here.'

'Here?' For the first time, Julius' eyes sharpened. 'What do you mean?'

She gave a soft, slightly embarrassed laugh. 'When you read the details, you will see. I believe they give us some important and interesting links. There is no doubt that the Bernard family knew Ravel; the question is, did they know him well enough to be given such a piece of work? And if so, is it the sonata we know as *Le Gouffre*?' She handed the document case to Julius, who took it with his slightly trembling hands. She thought of the excitement he would feel when he realised how close they were coming to the truth, and smiled. But he looked grave, and slowly unfolded the flap of the case. Beside him, Geoffrey Zauber, his big hands resting easily on his equally big thighs, looked on expectantly.

EXTRACTS FROM RESEARCH NOTES OF SANDRINE DELAGE

Subject: BERNARD Augustine Marianne
Born: 8 February 1919, Bayonne, Basses-Pyrénées
Parents: BERNARD Charles-Joseph and ETCHEGARY Marie
Profession of father: Musician and journalist
Other children of marriage: Geneviève (born 1909, married Hervé Bitterman 1929, two children, deceased 1953 from long-standing illness); Claude (born 1912, never married, still alive)
Mother of subject died 1930, father in 1940. Subject lived in Biarritz till end of the war. In 1945, subject married Gordon Parker, an Australian who had served as a soldier in Europe, and went to Australia with him. Marriage ended in 1954. After this time, subject stayed in Australia, working as a piano teacher. Her nephew Lucien and niece Marie lived with her for a while after their mother's death.

Subject died in Sydney in 1993.

Although Claude Bernard is still alive in France, our attempts to contact him proved fruitless. He is very ill and now resides in a nursing home and is unable to cope with questions. We did, however, discover the following information about Geneviève's side of the family, as follows.

Subject: BITTERMAN Hervé Maurice
Born 2 March 1900, Paris, France, of parents of German nationality. They later took on French citizenship. Hervé Bitterman, after leaving school, worked in M. Bernard's music shop, where he met Geneviève. Not long after they were married, however, they moved to Paris to take up the lease on another music shop. Bitterman died in crossfire in Paris in the early days of the Occupation. His widow and children then moved back to the south.

Lucien and Marie Bitterman came to Australia in 1954, at the ages of 22 and 15, respectively. Both children were reputedly highly talented—Lucien as a writer and musician, Marie as a pianist—but both were also highly-strung (not surprising, given their rather traumatic childhoods). Lucien left Australia in 1956 to return to France, but died soon after, apparently by his own hand. Marie Bitterman stayed with her aunt and went to an Australian institution to study music. We have not been able to ascertain what happened to her after this, but it is believed she married.

Subject: BERNARD Charles-Joseph
Born: 4 September 1872, Toulouse, Haute-Garonne, France

Parents: BERNARD Jean-Pierre and CASSAGNE Marthe

Profession of father: Viticulturalist

Subject's mother was known as a singer in the Toulouse region, and it is believed to be from her that young Charles-Joseph got his musical talents and inclinations. Like many of his generation, he went to the Paris World Fair where he mingled with musicians and composers from all over the world. Perhaps it was here he met the young Ravel, like him a fascinated member of the audience for the Javanese and Balinese orchestras, which caused such a sensation. Subject moved to Biarritz at the age of twenty-five, in 1897, and obtained, at first, irregular work as a musician in the summer, then more regular work, including, eventually, that of music critic for local and national publications. He was especially interested in French music and its differences from, and similarities to, music composed in other parts of Europe at the time. He was also ahead of his time in declaring jazz to be a respectable and multi-layered idiom, this despite the fact that he had been trained classically. Subject married in 1905, at the age of 33. His wife was a Basque woman from Bayonne. Children born in 1909, 1912 and 1919. His wife died 10 years before him, and he lived with his daughter Augustine in their house in Biarritz until his death in 1940, at the age of 68.

In the library, Tom Rice scanned the microfich newspapers patiently. He was sure that somewhere would lie the one thing he had so far failed to pick up, the one thing that would lead him to an understanding of the connection between Newton and Pym. And some idea as to where Pym might be now—if he was not six feet under the ground, which felt more and more likely. Otherwise, why would he have disappeared so thoroughly? No-one had seen him at any of the places he was supposed to have frequented. It was just like a conjuring trick—now you see me, now you don't. Tom Rice smiled grimly to himself and kept reading, searching for that nugget of truth.

And suddenly, just as he'd almost given up, there it was. It was just a small interview on page six of one of the papers, obviously conducted when interest in the story had died down. The interviewer had asked Pym the question, 'Did you know Dr Newton before all this?' And Pym had replied, 'I had never met him. Not as such. I had read his books, of course. And I had heard about him from my family. They knew him, long before he was famous. And knowing him, they could hardly believe how famous he became.'

The stupid interviewer hadn't taken him up on that! Rice could not believe it. He ground his teeth in frustration. He glanced at the interviewer's name, and sighed. He knew the guy. Right. He got up, and went to make a phone call.

He was very thoughtful on the way home. The other journalist had not been very interested in checking his notes, and it was only when Rice promised to put him in touch with one of the protagonists in the Rossi case, to do a 'hindsight' sort of story, that he had deigned to go and look at them. Rice had waited for several minutes at the end of the phone, until finally the man had come back.

'Sorry mate, not got much there. Except for one small thing. Pym mentioned he was an only child, and that he'd lived in some northern suburb, I think it was Dinwood. He said he'd gone to the Catholic school there. That's all. Sorry. Why d'you want the info, anyway? The story's cold, isn't it?'

'Yeah,' Rice lied. 'Quite cold. But I'm writing a book on my stories.'

'I see.' Rice could hear the other man's smile. 'Best of luck then.' He paused, then in a matey burst, 'Almost not quite real, that Pym, know what I mean?'

Yes. Rice knew what he meant. In all the dealings he'd had with Pym, he had never once felt he knew the man. Not even superficially. He slid away from any attempt to place him, any attempt to get closer. Rice had not liked him. In fact, he'd been quite repelled by him, by the coldness of his eyes, and felt sorry, in a way, for Julius Newton. But nevertheless Newton had it coming to him. The man was altogether too sure of himself. He was one of those whatdoyoucallits, tall poppies, sacred monsters, whatever. You had to expose those sort.

Before he went home, he called in at the police station to see if anything had happened. The policeman at the counter looked at him patiently and said, 'I'm sorry, sir. Nothing as yet. But we are circulating the drawing of the missing person.' His tone said that the likelihood of tracking down just one more missing person out of the hundreds, thousands who disappeared each year was practically nil. At the beginning, they had even suggested Pym had voluntarily disappeared, though why he should want to do so, after inspiring such a blaze of publicity, was hard to fathom.

Back home, Rice cut himself a long-delayed sandwich and made himself a pot of tea while he thought about what he had so far. Not much; but he could start by checking the Catholic schools in Dinwood. That'd be a start, though a long shot indeed.

SIX

URGENT FAX TO TOM RICE

Tom, you probably know some of this. A man answering to the description of Charles Joseph Pym stayed at the Grevillea Boarding House last May. He gave his place of last residence as Bayonne, France. He left the boarding house in early July and has not returned.

Through a source, I was able to check immigration records and found that no-one of that name left the country this year—or the last. I am in the process of checking other sources.

All the best,
Terry

★

'Roxane, I listened to your tape. It was very brave of you ...'

'Oh yes?' Watchful eyes; a stillness.

'I'm sorry. I hope you don't think I … it was very painful to listen to. Yet somehow, it made my parents more real. More …' Awkwardly, Alex moved to her and touched her shoulder. 'It's strange, hearing those stories that I've half known. And hearing my parents, speaking again through you. It's odd, you know; I never considered how much their death hurt you. It was me, always me.'

'And why shouldn't it have been? Far greater a loss for you, for a child.' Roxane's eyes were suddenly bright. Perhaps it would not be so difficult after all, this change, perhaps all it required was willingness and courage. 'I know now that I was quite wrong, leaving you with Julius. But I was so caught up in my own misery … and I thought, He is young, he will grow and understand, eventually. Or maybe I didn't think at all. Julius and I … we're not used to thinking of others, you see.'

'That's not true. You do yourself an injustice.' His body was still, his every movement tuned to her, to making peace with the past. 'I think of poor Julius,' he said, at last. 'And it grieves me, to feel pity for him. He was always so strong, so sure.'

'Don't,' she cried. '*Don't* say that.'

'He has courage, though. More than I would have, in his situation.'

'I'm not sure if that is courage, Alex, or merely a kind of blindness. Emptiness, even. I'm not sure. Don't look at me like that. Children want everything to work out, I know; but Alex, what happened in your childhood really did happen. Don't reinvent it now.'

TAPE 2, Roxane Newton

Afternoon, and the house is quiet, so maybe I'll try this again. It is odd, I am almost eager, even though another part of me thinks, Who could possibly care? And yet, every day I see, at the newsagent's, magazines filled with stories about what someone said about someone, or how someone else had a hot fling, or a wild party, or a pet cat. It's odd; those people thrive on being material for gossip. They thrive on living out every small, embarrassing, boring detail on camera. I can't quite believe it's happened to us, or how easy it is to fall into the pattern. Maybe it's the godless form of confession. It absolves you of sin so you can go out and sin some more. Did you see the feature on Julius, last year, before all this blew up, in the *Stars Weekly*? Julius was chagrined but pleased, if that's possible. He's always maintained he despises such publications—but it's flattering to be thought of as a star! Even if it's a dwarf star, or an exploding one.

Back to my *moutons*, as Julius would say. You'll know by now it's the usual story: academic seduces female student, uses her, then dumps her. Except you'd be wrong. I was just as much seducer as seduced; and after a while I was quite aware of Martin's clay feet, and of the fact that he had entered into this affair with me principally to get access to Julius and his enviable media contacts. Martin did not see himself as a two-bit lecturer for ever; he saw himself as a man of destiny. I knew all that, very soon; yet though it made me more embarrassed than angry, I couldn't help keeping on seeing the man. There was something so terribly vulnerable about him; something soft and so self-centred that it was endearing. If you can understand that! He was like a child, I suppose: forceful and loved and unformed. How could he doubt himself? He had an adoring wife, adoring students, a lovely child, and ample opportunity to live a wonderful life. After the first couple of months, he took up with other girls, as well as me. He was a bit disconcerted by my lack of adoration; but eventually, I think, he came to see it as restful. He could talk to me frankly. As to me—well, at first, of course, I bled. I ached. But I think I'm quite a cold fish, at heart; I start to see things I shouldn't. Oh, I grew up alright during that time, and I'm grateful to Martin for that. I came to see myself clearly, and I wasn't always very pleased with what I saw. But at least I knew. I couldn't pretend any longer.

Six months after Martin had first bestowed his favours on me (what does that show, that I date things from that?), Alexander and Sarah were killed in a car crash, and you came to live with us. Alexander and I had not been as close as we were as children—that business with Julius had cast a chill—but his death was a fearful blow. I could hardly think or feel straight for months, for years. I wept for Sarah too—wept for them both, for what they'd had, what they could have had; wept long and selfishly and dreadfully for the loss of the one person who saw me clearly. Yes, I wept for you, my poor little Alex, too, for you are listening now, aren't you? I'm not sure if you remember it at all well, but I never seemed to stop crying at that time.

After that, you occupied much of my life. I still saw Martin and I was doing very well in my course and was expected to get high marks. And it was good to have an on-again, off-again relationship, though I noticed Martin seemed to be getting more restive. He reacted well to Alexander's death; that is, well for me. He did not attempt to 'communicate', to attempt to 'heal' me. He saw that I was deep in grief, and though it was not something he necessarily understood, he was clever enough to know not to probe. I was appallingly sensitive about it, it was like a deep bruise I carried about with me for years, and any pressure on it made me hit out instantly. So, horrifyingly, life went on. Every day, Alex, my dear Alex, I would look at you and see my brother and his wife, and a kind of furious disbelief would twist my guts.

Poor little Alex! I know I've said that a lot, but then again, it's true. Looking back on it, Julius and I, we had so little to give you. So little of what mattered. No wonder you married so young, though you were lucky. But then again, your father had married young; and had also been lucky. Sometimes, Alex—and perhaps this will hurt you—it seems to me that you and Isabelle have a burden. The burden of measuring up to a marriage that stays vivid in the memory, the union of your father and mother, a union not tested by the grinding of time. Or maybe you don't see it as a burden, you see it as an inspiration, and I am merely a withered spinster who never learnt to love properly.

So then. You have Julius, me, and you in the house where we'd recently moved. I used to go down to the city every so often to catch up on tutes and things. I'd transferred to an external degree and Martin had proven most helpful about giving me extra instruction—and extra other things, it goes without saying. I enjoyed both, in an angry sort of way. I wasn't angry with Martin, for who could be angry with a natural force? No, I was angry with life.

And then, well, things changed a bit. One morning, as I sat across the table from you, watching you gravely enjoying your breakfast, I felt an urge to have a child. There were my brother's eyes regarding me; eyes not in the tomb, but alive, his yet not his, layered with Sarah's glance as well. Coldly I thought, Martin's the one, I might not have another chance. And so ... well, it was easy enough. I just stopped the pill, not telling Martin, of course, and there I was. There I was.

Julius was furious. It surprised me, the way he carried on. It doesn't now. He hates things to be untidy, or ridiculous. It wasn't that he thought I was immoral; I was just being a bloody nuisance. And besides, I think he was panicked, thinking he'd have this pregnant woman in the house, getting visibly bigger, and all the messy rest of it. He offered to pay for an abortion, which I refused, coldly, with real revulsion. I could not understand how he could think of killing, after we'd had so much death in our family. And then he did the unforgivable. He rang Martin's wife.

Now, I'd never met her. I'd once caught a glimpse of a photo of her in Martin's office, and there was something about her that seemed faintly familiar, though I couldn't place her. And I didn't have a good chance to look, for Martin snatched the photo away and put it in the drawer of his desk. I suppose you could say that for him—he wanted to keep his lives separate. He would never say a bad word against her. Once he'd said she was musical, and was teaching their child herself, but that was all. I had no idea about anything else. He never even called her by name, he'd just say 'my wife'. The thought had occurred to me before that he was keeping her apart not only because he didn't want her to know about his philandering, but also to protect her, in some odd sort of way. Not saying her name was perhaps a superstitious device against letting any of his lovers get any power over her. I can't say I thought about her much; it's probably utterly reprehensible in these days of sisterhood, but I can't say I cared much. You can't really care about someone you've never met, have only caught a photographed glimpse of. It's like caring about a wraith. Sometimes I wasn't even sure she existed.

Why Julius thought contacting her would do any good, I don't know. But one day, I came home from one of my trips to the city to find an unfamiliar car parked outside the house. That was not a surprise; Julius often had callers. But as I approached the house, I had a strange feeling of terror, like hearing the dry rustle of a snake before you see it. I opened the door very quietly and went in. There were voices coming from the living room; or rather, there was Julius' voice, and a soft murmur underneath. I don't know where you were that day; I think Julius had sent you over to play at a friend's house. I walked very quietly along the hall, still hoping to stave off whatever it was in there. But Julius heard me. He called out, 'Ah, Roxane! Come here a moment.' There was no terror or even pain in his voice, though; there was only a firmness, and even a kind of relief.

She was standing there with the child, her back to me, but as I came in, she slowly turned around and looked at me. I remember thinking how thin she was, and how much the child looked like her, yet with Martin's hair, softer and paler though. Her eyes, like the child's, were very deep-set and dark. They showed little that I cared to recognise. She was dressed very smartly, everything layered carefully, gleaming, as if it had been painted on, rather than being organic things of flesh and blood and cloth and hair. She said nothing at all, just looked at me.

'This is Mrs Cosgrove,' Julius said gravely, so that I wanted to punch him, tear his hair out. The sudden violence inside me made me feel quite ill. I nodded. She just kept looking.

seven

Police Sergeant Colin Oxford was almost at the end of his shift. He hated being on desk duty, and today had been particularly bad. Which is to say, boring. So when he took the call from the woman with the rather funny accent, he listened with only half an ear, noting down what she said quite dutifully, but not taking much account of it. That was the trouble with missing person notifications—you got all kinds of false leads from people who imagined they'd seen the missing person in all kinds of places. But he wrote it all up carefully afterwards, and left it for his relief to find. She read it with little enthusiasm at first, but it was a slow day, and she went to see her superior about it. He read it too and agreed it might be of interest, and wheels started to turn. There would probably be nothing in it; but it was worthwhile at least putting out a tentative feeler or two.

Meanwhile, Tom Rice was having a frustrating afternoon. No-one in any of the Dinwood schools, Catholic or state, had heard of Charles Joseph Pym. He sat next to the phone, tapping on it with some impatience, trying to think. How would the mind of Pym work? Someone like that could not be trusted to tell the truth in any way, could they? Would any of their details not be open to doubt? He went back to that potboiler story of Poe's, trying desperately to cast himself into the mind-set of Pym. Turning it over, he came across the back cover blurb: 'Apart from its violence and mystery, the tale calls attention to the art of writing and to the problem of representing truth. Layer upon layer of elaborate hoaxes include its author's own role of posing as a ghost-writer of early portions of the narrative ...'

Posing as a ghostwriter ... Was the whole name, not just the Pym part, a concoction? Obviously! He could have kicked himself. He began leafing through the book, jotting names down at random. Ricketts. Augustus Barnard. Henderson. Dirk Peters. The name had to be there somewhere, Pym's real name. Somehow, it must be pieced together. Excitement chilled his spine. This was proving to be far bigger than he had ever imagined.

But why, in the first place, had Pym gone to Newton? Perhaps it would be better to approach things from that angle. Why hadn't he chosen some Ravel specialist in France? Presumably because they wouldn't have been taken in. But some of them had. It was a circular argument. But the particular malevolence of the hoax, the malevolence directed at Newton, had to have some explanation. He would have to go and see him. There was no doubt of that.

Isabelle and Alex always enjoyed the walk back from preschool with the children. Today was such a beautiful day, even better than usual. And the news was good; they had finally delivered their first joint manuscript to the publisher, who had seemed very pleased with it. So they held the twins' hands and jumped with them, playing the sorts of games which adults think they're exiled from, until they have children.

They had almost reached the gate of the house when they saw a police car draw up. Isabelle and Alex looked at each other and walked rapidly towards the house, still holding the hands of the twins, who, bewildered by their parents' change of mood, protested loudly. Alex thought of Roxane, alone in the house. But surely, surely, it was safe! Isabelle thought of Julius, and accidents. By the time they reached the gate, the police officer was walking up the path to the door.

'Good afternoon, sir, madam. Is this your residence?'

'Yes.' Alex's heart began thumping. Strange that when you saw the police, you immediately thought of the silly things you might have done, the odd joint smoked at parties, the odd packet of lollies pilfered at school, and somehow you imagined they could see right into you and would care about what they saw there. He remembered Julius saying once that uniforms were potent things; their inhabitants were flesh and blood and frail, but the uniforms had a life of their own.

The policeman consulted his notebook. 'You are Mr Alexander Newton?' Alex nodded. The twins, overwhelmed for a moment by the sight of the police, lost interest and went to hammer at the door.

'You have relatives staying with you, I believe?' Were they always so maddeningly slow? Alex wondered, panic rising in his throat. Isabelle looked at him, and their eyes spoke to each other.

'A Miss Roxane Newton and a Dr Julius Newton?'

For God's sake.

Roxane opened the door to the twins. She had opened her mouth to say something, but closed it again when she saw the group on the doorstep. The policeman acknowledged her with a nod and a 'Good afternoon, madam.'

She looked inquiringly at him. 'Good afternoon.'

'And you are Miss Roxane Newton?' Oh no, thought Alex despairingly, here we go all over again. He must have made some sort of sound, for the policeman looked at him, and he flushed a little.

'I understand you have recently come to stay here, with your brother, Dr Julius Newton?'

'Yes, that's right. Is Julius .... is he ...'

'Oh no, madam. Please reassure yourself. It is merely that we wish to speak with him.'

'Speak with him? Why, what about?'

'Just to clear up a small matter, madam,' said the policeman. 'I take it Dr Newton is not here at present?'

'No, he's out. He should be back this evening. Will I tell him ...'

'We would appreciate it if he would come down to the station. Some time. There's no rush. Nothing to worry about, just to clear up a small matter.' He smiled. 'I was on my way somewhere nearby, and I was asked to give the message. Thank you. Good afternoon everyone.' And with a nod, the policeman went back down the path, out the gate and back to his car.

The three of them stood there watching, unable to say a word. Then Isabelle said, 'Better go inside and see what the children are up to.' But the others didn't follow her. Aunt and nephew stood on the doorstep, looking at each other.

Alex shrugged. 'Probably nothing. There are any number of small infringements ...'

He knew that the police would not come round for a small infringement. But what on earth could Julius have got himself into? His mind jumped to the hoax. Had someone made a complaint about him? Perhaps Symphony Press had decided to sue, after all? But that would be through their solicitors, not the police. So ...

Roxane was shaking her head, her eyes cloudy. 'I cannot imagine ...' But Alex knew it wasn't that she couldn't, she just did not want to. 'Well, we can't stand here all day. We'll just have to wait till Julius gets back.'

He did not return till it was nearly dark, accompanied by Geoffrey Zauber and Sandrine Delage. Sandrine had asked to come with him—to tell the truth, she was curious about his family. She could not really imagine someone like Julius in the midst of the amiable chaos of family life. Geoffrey, however, had often visited Julius at home, and always enjoyed the experience.

There was an odd atmosphere here though. Zauber felt it almost at once, and knew that he must not linger too long, and must take the Delage woman back to her hotel. But she did not seem aware of any atmosphere, or if she did, was ignoring it, for she was talking brightly and cheerfully of what she had come to do. Her eyes often rested on Julius as she spoke, and she drew him often into the conversation, as if seeking his approval. Geoffrey smiled to himself. It looked like Julius hadn't lost his charm yet.

'It has been so marvellous for me, meeting Dr Newton,' Sandrine Delage was saying. 'His books were formative experiences for me. I have read them over and over! I remember particularly one passage, Dr Newton, it was in your Beethoven book, and I wrote it down and carried it around in my wallet for years. It so impressed me, it so expressed the soul of that man's music, for me.'

Julius smiled discreetly. He was looking rather tired, Geoffrey thought, from the position of his vigorous fifty years. Poor fellow, he was getting rather old. And Madame Delage was charming, but she was also very persistent. He said, 'Perhaps I should take you back, madame? You must be tired, after your long flight.'

She looked sharply at him, knowing what he was saying, but unwilling to end the day just there. 'I feel quite well, considering. But perhaps you are right. It has been a long day. For Dr Newton, too. But I have greatly enjoyed it, and hope to see you again soon.' She looked inquiringly at Julius. 'I will be here for about two weeks. We will, of course, meet again.'

'It has, indeed, been a great pleasure.' Julius' eyes were deep-shadowed, exhausted.

'And I will, on my side, with Mr Zauber's help, make inquiries about this Marie Bitterman.' She smiled. 'You see, we are getting closer to all the threads of this tangled tale, and it fills me with excitement to know that soon we will know the truth. That we will all understand that *Le Gouffre* is real, that it will take its place amongst Ravel's other immortal works!'

'But are you sure of that? It has definitely been proven?' Roxane asked.

'Oh, there are still one or two tests that must be done,' Sandrine acknowledged. 'But I am as sure of its genuineness as I am sure of ... of your Beethoven book, Dr Newton.' She smiled at Julius. 'And that was truly original.'

Julius said quietly, 'Your confidence in me overwhelms me, madame.'

There was definitely something in the air here, thought Geoffrey, but it had nothing to do with him. Quite firmly he said, 'We must go now. I will contact you soon, Julius. Good night all.'

He was aware Madame Delage was looking a little surprised, but he could not help that. Still, she made her goodbyes happily enough, and walked back to the car with him. She gave a delicate yawn, and rubbed at one eye. 'I think you are right, Monsieur Zauber. I am more tired than I realise. I have been kept upright by the adrenaline, I think.'

He smiled, and started the car. 'I know the feeling.'

'Dr Newton has a nice family. Strange he never married.' She said this quite unselfconsciously, and Geoffrey grinned to himself.

'Our Julius is not interested in *l'amour*, I think. He likes to write about it, to talk about it, but never in a physical way. But I don't believe he really understands it. He is too self-contained for that.'

'But have you read his Beethoven book? That was about one of the most passionate men ever! Yet Dr Newton was well able to capture his essence.'

'Well, yes.' He had not much liked the book himself, though of course it had become such a classic you could hardly say so. 'Julius is a good writer. He can imagine. But it does not apply to his real life, his real self.'

'Perhaps he has many selves.'

'Perhaps. Don't we all?'

'Dr Newton looked very tired,' she went on. 'One forgets that he is seventy, such is the quality of his mind.' She paused. 'In some ways, Mr Zauber, Dr Newton reminds me of Ravel himself. The same exquisite sensitivity, the same modesty, the same misunderstanding from ...'

Geoffrey glanced quickly at her. 'Julius is indeed an amazing man. But he has his faults, like everyone else.' He hesitated. 'I would not have said Julius has been misunderstood. This ... this latest problem has been most unfortunate, and most unfair, but you see, Julius has been in the public eye for a long time. And people are not forgiven for that.'

'Yes. Monsieur Zauber, do you believe you would have been taken in by Pym?'

'Quite possibly. And of course Julius wanted so to believe. He had to believe.'

'And now?'

'Well, madame, you should ask yourself that question, not me.'

'I *know* this sonata is genuine.'

'Julius also knew Pym was genuine.'

She looked at him quickly, nodded. 'That is going to be the problem, is it not, Monsieur Zauber? How will we convince people now that this is authentic Ravel?'

'You … er, we can only present the evidence we have. And so far, it looks good. We need to build a convincing case.'

'I am glad you say we, Monsieur Zauber. I wanted to present all this to Dr Newton because morally I felt this was the right thing to do. But I can see now that he is frail, perhaps too frail for such an undertaking.'

He looked at her and smiled ruefully. 'You must enlist better allies than me. People with more power and standing.' People, he thought, with more certainty. More stomach for this task.

'Oh, I will get those. But I think you believe, Monsieur Zauber. And I think that is most important. This will not be a fast thing, resolved overnight. It may take years.'

'I'm not sure if I'm up to that.'

She laid a hand on his arm. 'It is a worthwhile thing,' she said. Meeting her eyes, he was suddenly reminded of a photo of Ravel, taken in his last illness. It had illustrated the exquisite care Ravel took of his appearance: the silver-and-black hair brushed sleekly back; the perfection of line of suit, tie, shirt; the firm, closed mouth. And then the eyes: dark, sad, accepting, knowing, they stared out of the photo with intensity, yet also a gentleness he had never quite managed to fix. It was the face of a man who could be all things to all people, yet somehow still slip away from definitions and explanations.

'Yes, it *will* be a worthwhile thing.'

eight

'Will you accompany me, Alex?' Julius seldom asked for favours, and even now his tone was light. But his eyes belied it. He did not look like he had slept much recently.

'Of course.' If only they had been a demonstrative family. All that he could do now was to put on his coat and straighten his collar to indicate his readiness. Alex's throat burned with fear, but that, too, must not be shown. He said, 'Well then, may as well go.'

Julius was having trouble straightening his own coat, and he made no protest when Roxane helped him. She looked at him, and touched his arm gently, and Alex's heart contracted at the look in her eyes. No more pity there; they had gone beyond that, back to the original blood bond neither of them had acknowledged consciously before. What extremities we had to be driven to, to feel that, he thought, but there was no pleasure in the thought, no sense of new beginnings, just the knowledge that the grief would be sharper now because still it would not be spoken, only understood.

Julius' eyes lingered on his sister, then he nodded and, without a word, opened the door and stepped out into the deepening shadows of dusk. 'We'll take the car,' Alex said. 'You look tired.'

Julius nodded, again without speaking, and settled himself into the front passenger seat. The two women watched them go, each man careful with his own movements, careful not to infringe on each other's space, but with that space trembling between them.

It was when they were almost at the station that Julius pulled an envelope out of his pocket. 'Madame Delage gave me a copy of these, Alex. Perhaps you might want to read them later.'

He put the envelope on the dashboard and turned to face Alex, his eyes empty of all except a terrifying weariness. 'Whatever happens down there—just remember, the sonata is real. It's the truth. The only truth.'

Tom Rice wondered whether he should go to the police now with the information that had so amazingly dropped into his lap. The click as the phone engaged, the remembered, precise tones, the unseen smile in the voice. And what it had had to say! He had Newton now. Over a barrel. He debated with himself the necessity of informing the police. They wouldn't be interested particularly, except insofar as they had to amend their files. He could sit on this for a while, but not for long. And he knew from experience that the police were not apt to look kindly on the wasting of their time. He didn't have to tell them absolutely everything, just the main gist. He would sit on the rest. After all, it didn't concern them. Not really.

He arrived at the station just as a car pulled up outside. The car door opened, and, to his amazement, out stepped Julius Newton. Rice watched, pulling discreetly back as Newton levered himself stiffly upright and waited for another, younger man—the nephew, probably—to come around to him. Then the two of them went up the steps and into the station together. Rice followed them slowly. He had to know just what Newton was doing here, but he did not want them to see him just yet. He watched the pair talking to the desk sergeant, then watched as another policeman emerged and came towards them. He watched as they followed him out of sight. He would not go in, just yet, himself. He would wait until they re-emerged, and get some answers from them before he spoke to the police. He was a patient man. He could sit here for hours, if need be. Especially now.

The detective who sat opposite them was tall, smooth-skinned, blank-faced. His eyes were of a cold shining blue. He smiled at them, as he had smiled when Julius asked if Alex could come in with him. 'If you wish.' His tone, his smile conveyed friendliness, but behind the brightness of his eyes was something else. In fact, he was rather bored by this inconsequential task, but determined to extract what interest he could from it.

'Dr Newton, you are doubtless wondering why you are here.' Interesting, the old man's obvious discomposure. It made him wonder if there was anything in this ...

Alex watched as Julius gently shook his head. Somehow, it was not a surprise. But the detective's eyes sparkled.

'It will not come as a surprise then, sir, that Mr Charles Joseph Pym has been listed as a missing person?'

Julius said nothing, just stared at him, his hands twitching slightly.

The detective watched him for a moment, then said, 'When he was listed as missing, it was pointed out to us that Mr Pym might have enemies. It was also pointed out that he had no reason to disappear.'

Now Julius watched him, his hands still, his whole body rigid. Whatever Alex had expected, it was not this. Inside his throat, something fluttered uncontrollably. He hoped it would stop, or he might be sick.

'But many people disappear voluntarily. We know that. Most of the cases we are notified of turn out to be voluntary, although families do not always appreciate finding this out. But in Mr Pym's case, we checked. He appears to have no family. He vanished from the boarding house where he lived previously. He does not appear to have left the country. And yesterday, we received a call from an informant who told us that she saw Mr Pym some months ago, *after* the hoax was exposed, having lunch in a restaurant, with an older man. A man she described as very elegant, with neatly brushed silver hair and beautiful hands. She said she notices such things.' There was no mistaking the tone of the detective's voice now. 'But more than this. She said she knew the person Mr Pym was lunching with. She had seen him many times on TV, she said. He was one of her heroes. She said he was arguing, shouting at Mr Pym.' He looked at Julius, who bowed his head. 'I don't think I need to tell you, Dr Newton, who she was referring to.'

Alex looked at Julius, and saw that his shoulders were shaking. The flutter in Alex's throat reached up his chin and into his face.

'Dr Newton.' The detective leant forward. 'Since then Mr Pym has been listed as missing. Can you tell us what happened at that meeting?'

Julius slowly lifted his head. The shaking in his shoulders had subsided and he was terribly still. He looked back at the detective. When he spoke, his voice was very clear. 'Mr Pym and I had much to say to each other.'

'Really?' said the detective. 'I would have thought you had nothing to say to him. Hadn't he just made a fool of you by hoaxing you? Hadn't he just destroyed your career? You had always refused to speak to him through the media. Why did you meet him in person?'

'I don't think you understand. I had no choice.'

'No choice? What more could he do?'

The flutter filled Alex's face, behind his eyes, his nose, his mouth. But he could not move, or make a sound.

'What did you talk about?' the detective said to Julius' silence. 'Did he threaten you?'

Julius spoke at last. 'Oh no. He did not have to. His mere presence was enough.'

The detective's eyes sharpened. 'His mere presence was enough!' He leant back. This was proving to be more entertaining than he had imagined. 'Enough to be rid of it—for good?'

An idle shot, for there was nothing to indicate anything as extreme as that, but it went home. He saw the old man visibly wince and draw in on himself.

'My uncle is tired,' Alex burst out. 'Old. And you have no right to ask these sorts of questions, to imply the kinds of things you have been implying. You have not even cautioned him.'

'Cautioned him? When all we're doing is having a little chat? Well? Is that necessary? Dr Newton?'

For a long moment, Julius looked at him. Then, without glancing at Alex, he shook his head.

'But Julius! You know what he's saying, what he's driving at, don't you?'

But Julius did not protest. He did not cry out. He just shook his head very slowly.

'You see, I know that Pym will never come back. He never existed in the first place.' His shoulders started shaking again, but this time both of them saw clearly what was happening. Julius was laughing. Laughing! Laughing without any mirth, his eyes desperate. 'Murder! If there was any murder done—of identity, of truth— it was done by Pym.' He looked at the other two, rigid on their chairs. 'Read your Poe again.'

'Dr Newton, am I to take it that you are saying there was no Pym?'

'That's right.'

'But he was seen by many people, including your own family. He collaborated with you, Dr Newton. Are you saying you dealt with a nonexistent person?' The detective was struggling to keep his anger in check.

'Not at first. At first, I believed. But he soon made it his business to let me know where matters really stood.'

'You mean Pym himself was a hoax? An invention?' Alex could not control the fluttering at his lips, which at any moment threatened to overwhelm him.

'Yes. That's what I'm saying.'

'But, Julius ... if you knew, why did you let him ... why did you say ...'

'The sonata was real.' His voice firmed, and Alex suddenly thought how odd his choice of words was. 'It was real. He just ... he just padded it out with other things. I told you there was murder done. A murder of truth, of integrity, of beauty. He was ready to destroy all that for a moment of revenge. And now ... now I suppose he just wants to prolong the pleasure of it.'

'Revenge?' The detective leant forward.

'Revenge ...' Julius' voice sank to a whisper. His face was grey. '"I have graven it within the hills, and my vengeance upon ..."'

'Dr Newton, you must tell us. Who was this man Pym, if he was not what he claimed to be? And why did he want revenge? And why did you let him take you in? And where is he now?'

Julius stared at him. 'I do not know. I truthfully do not know. I have no answers. Except ...'

The detective was perfectly still. 'What do you mean?'

And so Julius told them.

TAPE 3, Roxane Newton

She was standing there with the child, her back to me, but as I came in, she slowly turned around and looked at me. I remember thinking how thin she was, and how much the child looked like her, yet with Martin's hair, softer and paler though. Her eyes, like the child's, were very deep-set and dark. They showed little that I cared to recognise. She was dressed very smartly, everything layered carefully, gleaming, as if it had been painted on, rather than being organic things of flesh and blood and cloth and hair. She said nothing at all, just looked at me.

'This is Mrs Cosgrove,' Julius said gravely, so that I wanted to punch him, tear his hair out. The sudden violence inside me made me feel quite ill. I nodded. She just kept looking.

'I have told her, and she agrees that ...' Julius was going on and on, unbelievably, prattling about the right thing to do, the right thing in the circumstances, and Martin's wife and I just kept looking at each other. Once again, I was struck by some familiarity about her, though I still couldn't place it. Now, although I was determined that I would have the child and that no-one should stop me, I felt a yawning horror open in me. This woman standing before me, with her silent child, was not at all what I had imagined. At the back of my mind had been a picture of a pretty, blonde, smiling little housewife who played tennis and was a whizz at making sandwiches for the canteen at school. Martin went home to that every night, I'd told myself, the aproned, efficient security every man wants. But this woman looked as if life itself was draining out through her hollow cheeks and her pale hair and dark eyes; the gleaming patina on her wasn't enough to hide the skeletal burning of her soul.

At length, Julius stopped talking, alerted by the strange quality of the silence. He waved his hands a little and said, 'Well, there we are,' and tried to smile. She turned her gaze on him. Then, at last, she spoke. She said, her eyes fixed on him, not on me, 'I don't think it's any use, do you, Dr Newton? Judgments have already been made. And now we are rushing into the embraces of the cataract, where a chasm throws itself open to receive us.' I remember thinking at the time that it was an odd, a very odd thing to say, but then everything about this situation, this woman, was. I thought, I knew then, that she was mad. She said, 'Poor Martin. He thought he was going to get something out of this,' and she laughed. It was not pretty.

'It's all over,' I found tongue to say at last. 'It really is. I promise.' She looked at me, her gaze flickering, testing, knowing I was saying that I would have the child, but that Martin was hers again. Then her gaze went back to Julius.

'Martin and I and our child, we're going away,' she said. 'There's another university' Then she smiled again, mirthlessly. 'But why am I telling you this?'

Julius, for once, was struck dumb. She patted her hair in a parody of tidiness and said, 'Well, goodbye. I don't suppose we will meet yet again.' She took her child's hand, and walked to the door. Then she paused, hesitated, turned, and looked at us again. She looked at me, especially. She said, 'I don't know why I thought you'd remember. I don't know what I thought.'

Something in her gaze, her words, made memory stir deep inside me, and I almost cried out. But I didn't. I couldn't. I stood there and watched her walk down the steps and out through the gate, on to the street. It was only then that it struck me that she had driven a long way for such a hideous interview. I shuddered uncontrollably. So this was to be my punishment. But for God's sake, it was hers too! Hers! How could she rip her heart apart so, how could she? I thought of Martin's uncharacteristic attitude towards her and, for the first time, I really loved him for something other than his lovemaking or his glamour, things that had long since faded. But if he'd known, why then had he ... Could it be that he'd thought of her, not of him? But then Martin was at heart a shallow creature, even if he did have good impulses. Perhaps he had the ability to put his feelings into separate boxes, and ignore one day what he'd known the day before.

Julius and I were left looking at each other. Then he smiled a little, and said, 'There is something very odd about that woman. Why should you remember her, when we'd never seen her before in our lives? I pity Cosgrove.' His eyes were uneasy; as if the woman had touched some nerve.

I said nothing. I had known from the moment I walked in the door and seen her there that I couldn't stay in that house, not after what he had done, to me, to her even.

'Now,' Julius said, 'what are we going to do about your situation?'

I said, 'My situation is solved, Julius. You won't have me cluttering up your house much longer. I'm leaving.'

'Leaving? Where? Why? What about Alex? How will I cope?'

I wished I could hate him. It would seem so much easier then. But in his eyes I saw the Julius of long ago, so easily disconcerted by our games, our tricks. I was suddenly overwhelmed by a weary pity. 'Don't worry, Julius, I'll make sure things are properly organised. But I think it's best if I do go. I think we could end up hating each other if I stayed. And I don't think I'll be of much use to Alex, in this state.'

He opened his mouth, then closed it. Julius may be obtuse, or pretend to be, but he's not stupid. He nodded, and I went away, already feeling guilty for abandoning you. But there was no way out. I could not stay.

I suppose you could say, how could I come back then, after this? Well, I'm sorry to tread on your dreams, but time softens all things. You have to care to keep those kinds of memories alive and bleeding. And I suppose I do not care enough, anymore. It's not only Julius who is getting older. It's me too. After all, Julius and I know each other in a way that not even my own son can know me, or I him. It's not even a question of forgiveness anymore, because for true forgiveness you need true remorse on the other person's side. It's just weariness, I suppose. Weariness, and that knowledge of each other. But that's by the by ...

Telling you this has made me think about it all again, has made that woman's face appear in my mind again. A strange face; not easily forgotten, but the details of which I have mislaid. And that strange feeling of having met her before ... But that was probably due to the heightened feelings that day; to my pregnant state too—the way I felt in those days as if I lived inside some kind of tragic story. I never spoke to Julius about her again, never. He was pleased about that, I am sure.

The tape clicked to a stop.

'I never got any further.' Roxane was sitting on the couch, looking at her hands as if they could tell her something. 'Her name was Mary, you know, Isabelle. Mary Cosgrove. I had never met her before, I am sure of that. But something about her reminds me of something ... And that strange thing she said, it's like ... like ...' She looked at Isabelle, a pulse fluttering uncontrollably in her throat. 'Isabelle, that letter, the one

Ravel was supposed to have sent, that quote from Poe, it was ...'

The two women looked at each other, a terrible chill gripping them. 'Martin would know,' Isabelle said suddenly. 'Wouldn't he? He would know who she was, what happened to her, whether any of this can have anything to do with ...'

'You can't mean ... I haven't spoken to Martin in years, decades. Seth meets him often, of course ...'

Isabelle kept looking at her. Roxane sighed. Her face was blotchy with tension, her hair awry. She said quietly, 'I don't know if I could bear it, talking to him ...' She got up, and moved to the phone. 'I don't even know if he's still at the university there ...'

Watching her, Isabelle knew that Roxane knew exactly where Martin was, had been keeping track of him for years. Yet she had never contacted him directly. What manner of woman was this, who could keep the passion and hate and grief of her heart locked up so securely? She felt a great surge of compassion, a compassion that was almost love, and that was certainly a long way from certainty. 'Ring him,' she said gently.

Roxane's fingers punched out the numbers without her looking at them, her face acknowledging the truth of her knowledge of Martin.

The phone was answered almost immediately, and Isabelle walked away. She had no wish to intrude on this. She would go and see once more if the children were asleep. In their quiet bedroom, filled with the scent of their bodies, the sweetness of their limbs, she sat down and cried with a grief such as she had never known, a grief for the sadness, the waste, the failure, the pain. A curiously painful grief, for it was unselfish, almost impersonal, unbearable in its inexorability.

Rice was getting rather stiff. With every minute that passed, he was re-assessing his ideas. He had thought of the possibility of Newton murdering Pym quite a while back, and indeed had worked from that basis for some time. But the information he'd received this afternoon had caused him to think again. Especially if Newton were up to his old tricks, trying still to pass off a forgery as the real thing! When he finally saw Alex and Julius emerging from the police station, he could not prevent a great bound of impatience, and raced to reach their car before they got in.

'Dr Newton! Dr Newton!'

Alex turned and saw him. He shouted, 'Why don't you bugger off? You've done enough harm, you bloody vulture.'

Julius turned too.

'Come on, Julius, let's go. We have no business with this man.'

'Pym rang me this afternoon,' Rice shouted. 'He told me what you're up to, Newton. He told me you and he had set the hoax up together. He told me you were trying to get the whole thing rolling again. He told me to tell you he's still there. He'll always be there.'

'You're behind the times, Rice,' Alex said, trembling. He helped his silent uncle into the car and shut the door. 'You don't know what you're talking about.' He went around to the driver's seat and got in.

Rice yelled, 'Don't think you can just get away with it, Newton. I know why you were at the police station. But I know more than they do. I know that this hoax was really yours. I know, Dr Newton, and I'm writing about it! Talk to me, or you may find yourself sunk for ever, because I don't need you, Newton. You need me!'

He rapped on the windscreen, but Alex started the car, and engaged first gear. Rice kept shouting, but they could only dully make out his words, and soon they had left him far behind.

nine

You don't understand, do you? None of you do. You all look at me with those frozen expressions, as if I've turned into a monster in front of your eyes. And maybe I have. A monster worthy of Poe. But it didn't start like that. It started so stupidly, you see.

When we look at the past, we writers, we see it as a story, something complete and coherent, something in which threads can be discerned. And so, in that story you call the past, the first spools were unwound years ago, and down through the past they came, tangling all the way, knotting further and further together. But what if the past is not a story? What if it is as savage and confusing as the present? What if we learn nothing from it? If we truly felt that, perhaps that would put us writers out of business, for what would it all mean then?

You don't want philosophical statements, I can see that on your faces. You want to know why. You want explanations. For God's sake, Julius. For God's sake. Explanations. Tell us!

But, you see, I didn't see it until it was all too late.

I suppose you could say it started years and years ago, when I was still a young man, not long after the war. Those were good times, exciting ones; don't ever let people tell you the fifties were boring. They were wonderful. Exhilarating. We had been through hideousness into something new. And we were determined to change things. I'm often amused by the insistence of the sixties generation that they changed things. Wrong. It was us, who had been through the war, who knew that things could not stay as they had been. And for people like me, that meant all kinds of immense possibilities opening; being able to be myself, at last.

It was the time when I discovered that I was a good writer; discovered, too, my fascination with the lives of musicians, with what made them different from other people. I had decided to start on a life of Beethoven; I had never read one that made me satisfied, that made me feel I was inside the icy grandeur, the flayedness, of his music. I felt overwhelmed by deciding this; I could hardly have chosen someone more different to me. And so I read, and thought, and talked furiously.

You know of course that I had many friends in those days, people I'd met during the war, who had emigrated. One such was a Frenchwoman who had married an Australian soldier called Gordon Parker, after the war. I'd met her in Biarritz, just after the war; she was a nice woman, and for a time I think she thought ... but no matter. Augustine, her name was. When I met her again in Australia, she had relatives staying with her, her niece and nephew. I believe they had had a hard time growing up; their father, who was French but whose parents were of German origin, had died during the war, caught in a bit of crossfire in the street, because someone took him for a German, I believe. Their mother, who was quite ill, died shortly after the war, so Augustine was *in loco parentis*, as it were. So I had sympathy, but you understand, I had not had a particularly easy time of it as a youth myself, and I felt impatient with the atmosphere of doom that hung around these two, the girl and the boy.

The boy, particularly—I call him boy, though he was a young man—was a difficult character. He was a tormented soul; very artistic, but unable to settle to anything. He modelled himself on Baudelaire, I believe; he saw himself as the albatross in that famous poem, the one who soars in the air but waddles on the ground, you know, the romantic vision of the artist. The girl was more ordinary; she played the piano well, but without any real understanding, I think. But she worshipped her brother; sometimes I think that was his real problem. She had made him believe he was a misplaced genius, whereas he could have lived quite happily if he had not had those expectations.

Augustine herself had no inkling of these things; she was a very nice, musical, but rather sentimental woman. She would come to my place with them and talk for hours about all the great men she had known; yes, including Maurice Ravel. She hinted at secrets she had, but I did not take her seriously; she was just that sort of woman. The two young people would sit there and listen, and I would try and engage them in conversation, but always they were so intense, it ruffled me, although Augustine tried valiantly to enter into the spirit of things.

One day, I spoke about my Beethoven project, and her eyes lit up. 'Oh, monsieur, did you know that Lucien here has written the beginnings of a very marvellous dissertation on that most angelic of composers!' I wasn't really interested; the young man was, as I've said, a rather difficult person whose type did not really attract me. And in any case she was an amateur and probably foolish enough to believe in Lucien's own image of himself. I had already published many articles, and made a name for myself. Despite my obvious lack of interest, she brought it the next week, and I promised I'd read it. Well, the week had almost passed before I glanced at it; I thought I'd better do so, in case she asked a tiresome question about it. So I opened it reluctantly—and was immediately riveted.

It was extraordinary, there was simply no doubt about it. It gave a completely new interpretation of the character of Beethoven, of his life yet not his work. There was nothing in it about 'that most angelic of composers', as that silly woman had said. This was something quite different; something written in a kind of cold fury, yet with a rightness I could hardly bear. Lucien's Beethoven carried the abyss within him, so strongly ... As I read it, I remember the rushing of my pulse, the knowledge that never would I have been able to articulate what he had. It filled me with an excitement that was close to panic, I remember; a kind of heating of the blood that made me feel faint.

But my book was already contracted. I was to start work. What could I do? I gave the manuscript back to Lucien, with a neutral comment like, 'Interesting.' He looked at me then, I remember, and there was a strange expression in his eyes. I believe he had expectations of me. So many people did, you know. And I've tried to give people what they want without compromising myself too much ... But in this case, you see, I could do nothing. Literally. I simply couldn't. But he said nothing to my polite excuses. His sister wasn't there that day, I can't remember why.

After that, somehow, I didn't see Augustine or her relatives much; I was told she had moved to another city with her husband, and the young people had returned to France. I had no idea what happened to them. And why should I? I had had, as I said, precious little real contact with those two young people, and I must say I was relieved to find them out of my life.

I know what you're going to say; I can read your stricken eyes. Julius, you copied! You stole, Julius. For those insights, those terrifying phrases are in the book, are they not? And how could they not be? They were burned into my brain. I could no more not use them than I could stop breathing. They were what I had wanted to reach; they were the truth.

I'm not ashamed of what I did. I knew my work was important. And it was only a part, what that boy had written. Only a small part. He would never have done anything with it, I knew he just did not have the strength to build on that. His kind of passion burns itself out without leaving anything behind. He would become a defeated man, an ordinary man living in a suburb somewhere. I knew that magnificence would stay buried forever. In many ways, it was an act of kindness, of selflessness. I rescued his thoughts from obscurity.

I knew those people would never challenge anything; they were simple people, in many ways. And as time passed, I knew I was right. No-one came forward to challenge, to accuse. That young man didn't even have the spine for that. And besides, I had made the work my own; I had clothed it in my own insights, my own being. It was mine.

Now you've confused me. I can't see my way forward. I can only tell you what happened, when Pym contacted me. Not long after he'd read the umpteenth edition of my Beethoven book, I understand. There was an odd tone to our communications after that, but I did not understand or concern myself unduly. When I met him ... why, you were there, you were all there. You saw what he was like. Perhaps you could not understand my reaction to him. But you see, from the beginning, he told me he knew. Told me he'd known the real author of those passages in the Beethoven book, knew how to contact him, that he now needed my help to publicise his find, and that of course I would help him. I didn't ask any questions. I knew I had done the right thing, but would the world see it like that? The world frequently does not weigh up things in the balance, does not recognise complexities; it frequently prefers to make up its mind, irrespective of circumstances.

I had no idea what Pym's connection was to that long-ago young man, I only knew that somehow, he knew. He talked to me of Lucien, over and over, but his pictures of him were strange, skewed, as if Lucien was no more than an icon to him, without humanity or contradictions. His vengeance was not for Lucien, it seemed to me; and I could not understand it, but I accepted it somehow, without question.

And he laughed, you know, when he told me. 'All those years, the sword hanging, and you never knew!' He said that the intention had been there, always. And that he knew he was absolutely right, that all doubts disappeared when he heard me speaking on the radio, you remember, just before the birthday party, Alex. He said then, 'You spoke about that meeting on the beach as if you truly did not remember whom you had met. You spoke as if they advanced the great cause of Julius Newton, as if those three had no existence save the one you gave them in your vignette!'

Of course, it had been Augustine and her niece and nephew, there on the beach, long ago. That was how I met them. But why did I have to mention that? It wasn't important. They were representatives of France as a whole. I didn't rise to his bait; I said nothing. I didn't ask him anything; there was no need. I suppose it was like placating a Fury; you know, if you have the right rituals, if you don't speak its name aloud ...

And besides, the things he had to show me were extraordinary. Not the letter, the photo; but the sonata, yes, and the story about Ravel's relationship with Marta Susskind. That had the smell of truth, of some kind of truth, I still believe that. He told me he'd got it from an old woman who had once known Ravel, and I believed him. He didn't say it was Augustine, but I thought it probably was. I didn't ask any more; in some ways it is true, what he said. I really wanted to believe in this; I have always felt a kinship to Ravel, who was so out of place in our gross, extravagant century, who did not declare himself except through his music.

Why should I, you might ask, in the circumstances, believe the sonata was genuine? Well, like Madame Delage, I just recognised Ravel's unmistakeable imprint on this. I knew the letter and the photo were more of a problem; they were possible, but not probable. Just as Marta herself was possible. But the music ... ah, the music! Either this young man was the world's most accomplished composer, or else this was the genuine article.

And I soon realised that he was a good musician, but that he had no real creativity of his own. He was always too intent on making an impression, on playing the part of my Nemesis. There was a blankness in him, a cold centre, that would have prevented him from writing anything true, for an artist must write from himself, must he not, from the truth of him.

And you might think I am not one to talk of the heart, but I truly loved that music. It truly spoke to me.

I felt anything was worth it, to bring that music to the world. And I wanted to be the one to do it. That is the hideous thing; that Pym cared so little, oh not for me, but for the music, for that anguished composer who was Ravel, and even, you know, even for that ridiculous but perhaps deeply pathetic young man, Lucien. That is what I did not understand, and still can't. There was no love in his portrayal of Lucien; there was just a kind of incantation, as if he were calling up some ritualised god. I tell you, at some times I seriously considered whether he was mad. Not mad in the way we normally see it, as a vivid, distorted presence; but madness as a kind of absence, a lack of anything at all, so that I even came to see him, as I've said, as a kind of Fury, an alien.

What were my feelings? What can you expect? On the one hand, I was excited about the Ravel book, and considered Pym a small price to pay. On the other, at a deeper level, I was fearfully uneasy. I knew things could not last like this. But I had no idea Pym would do what he did. If I had, I would certainly never have gone ahead with it, any of it. I would simply have got the sonata authenticated. I thought ... well, I thought he would be content just to have this power over me, this knowledge. After all, why would I think otherwise? In exposing me, in conducting this cruel hoax—a double one, for he succeeded in obscuring the music— he would be exposing himself, too. Who would take him seriously after such a thing? People are afraid of hoaxers, you know, because in their very coldness they repel.

Well, you know what happened. I don't need to tell you.

I don't need to tell you the agonies I suffered, the horrible humiliation. Maybe I had been wrong, taking Lucien's words; but surely it did not merit this dreadful revenge? And besides, I had told him I was willing to put an acknowledgment of help from Lucien Bitterman, something like that, in the next edition of the book. It wasn't enough for him.

Yes, I met him that last day, the day he was supposed to have disappeared. He contacted me and said we should meet, that we still had much to discuss, and then he laughed, and I knew the threat was still there, and that this time he would destroy me utterly, or else stay in my life like a time bomb. I just asked him, please, to tell me if there had been any truth in it, anything at all, and he just smiled and said I would never know. I did not ask myself his motives, and I know you will think that's odd. At the beginning, I had imagined he might be Lucien, but I knew he wasn't—he was too young for that. In a way, I suppose I thought he was Nemesis. I had had a charmed life, a good one. It could not last.

That day, that last day I saw him, he did not tell me any more; he just talked inconsequentially, as if we were civil acquaintances. Except for one moment, one moment when he looked at me, smiled and said, 'Some lives, some families are bound as tightly as a jigsaw puzzle, don't you find, Dr Newton?' He leant back, looked at me, smiled. And then he began talking about the music, going over its points as if none of this had happened. That was when I was sure he was crazy; and that the music was real too. He as much as admitted to that, you see, I'm sure of that. And all that detail about Marta, about that time: it was too real, too vivid, to be completely made up. Someone must have told him, there must have been something in it.

I tried to ask him again, saying didn't he care about beauty, about truth, about music, about anything at all, something for the sake of Ravel, even? That is what I meant by murder. And Pym laughed then without answering me and said that he was leaving my life, leaving it like his namesake did, in that wretched tale of Poe's, sailing away into the blankness of unwritten pages. And I would never know. Would never understand what had driven him. Would never know why the revenge, the malice, had to be so complete that even that wonderful music had to be sacrificed to it. For this was music that had stared into the abyss, and knew it intimately, yet had never given in to it. It had to be Ravel's, with his exquisite, sorrowful sensibility; it could not have been Pym's: for you see, Pym *was* the abyss, as blank as that. And the abyss cannot write itself.

It is like that story of Poe's, you know, no, not the Pym one. That one about the man approaching the whirlpool, an abyss he cannot escape. I was being drawn closer and closer to its lip and there was no way I could draw back. No way. When Madame Delage contacted me, I felt as though the whirlpool, which had suddenly stopped, was spinning faster again. Yet I was powerless to do anything. And I have always believed in the sonata. I have always believed in the beauty and truth of composers' works. I have always believed—and I think that has been my achievement. I think that even after all this, that may remain. Surely that will be allowed to remain. Surely this one small lapse will not be allowed to destroy everything. It is not just me, my work, that is being destroyed. Remember that. It is trust. It is the memory of pleasure, the pleasure of my readers. It is the pleasure of communication. I may have plagiarised; but it was an impulse. Just a momentary lapse. Think of that, and have mercy.

ten

'We rang Martin, Julius.'

'Martin?'

'My son's father. Remember? Martin Cosgrove?'

Had they all gone mad? Wasn't it enough, that the abyss had opened before him, before them? Did they have to confuse him as well? Of course, they had never understood him really, no-one had, ever. Lucien—he remembers Lucien, he hasn't told them everything, but he can't. Anyway, there is nothing to tell, nothing left. It had all been a mistake, an aberration. Not even Pym had said ... No, there was nothing except the faded memory of those eyes. And who knows what was really in them?

'He had a wife, Julius. Martin, I mean.' Why is her face so soft, wobbling, her eyes accusing? He has confessed all that matters, all that is real, surely he is entitled to something, something ...

'I remember, just about. Yes. A very strange woman. Probably mad.'

'She is dead now.'

He does not answer that. What possible business is it of his? Why are they not comforting him, understanding? Or, if not, confronting? He could take either, but this ... Why are they all looking at him like that, so still?

'She died in a mental hospital in 1976.'

'Very sad for Cosgrove.' He has decided to humour her.

'Julius, her name was Mary. But her maiden name was Bitterman. Marie Bitterman.'

He can hardly breathe, though the name whirls in his mind. He looks at her, and an image floods his mind, not of a real person, but that one Pym had given him. *Marta Susskind. Marie Bitterman.* The thought made him breathless. Of course, she had not looked like Lucien, they were like chalk and cheese, but he'd had the girl in his house many times. Why hadn't he recognised her? Of course, people change a lot, and she more than anyone. He thought of her as she had been, small, insubstantial, and then that woman, so gilded, so groomed ... Marie and Lucien. The two of them. Yes. No wonder they hated the Newtons. The brother had his work taken from him; the sister, her husband. At least, that was how they would see it, that was how their crippled minds would have constructed it. But any normal person would have resisted ... it wasn't his fault. Lucien could have said ... Nothing had been said, acknowledged. And why hadn't she, Mary, done anything? Why wait all this time? He sits down slowly, carefully, his eyes fixed on Roxane. 'Oh, my God.'

Roxane says nothing. Her eyes are full of a strange emotion he can't put a name to. Behind her, Isabelle and Alex watch them both, their shoulders close to each other, just touching. He can see Alex's eyes on him; these are things his nephew did not know, things entering coldly into his heart. But Julius cannot think of that; he is veritably fighting for his life now.

'Martin said Mary had always been a strange woman. He said she had never recovered from her brother's death. He killed himself, you know? He said that her need was so great that he, Martin, could not fill it ...' She stops, thinking of Martin's voice, the pain in it, the softness she had never wanted to acknowledge, and Julius winces at what he takes to be her contempt. 'Those two, Lucien and Marie, had had, as you say, a difficult childhood. But they were devoted to each other, they clung to each other, they were a world unto each other. Martin did not know the full story, but he knew Marie hated us. Marie had not told him why she hated you, Julius, and he assumed it was because of me. She was mad, yes, Julius, in that way you described ... a vivid presence, was that it? Oh yes, that presence was vivid enough in their home.'

He has his head in his hands now, and he is shaking. He is thinking of Lucien, remembering even the look of those words he had written—the cramped, angular letters—and the look in his blue eyes as Julius handed the pages back, the touch of his soft, dry hand.

A terrifying surge of an emotion he cannot yet place sweeps through him, so that he shouts as if he were in pain. 'But he is dead, long ago. And she is dead too, you say. *Dead*. So it cannot be her ...'

Roxane looks at him. She can hear the sorrow of Alex and Isabelle, behind her, she can feel it radiating in waves around her. But she can't quite feel, herself, yet. 'Martin said Mary talked a lot about her aunt, Augustine. She said she had known Ravel. She liked to talk of her aunt's past, because it was happy, she said, because it was like a picture she could hold in her hands and study. She hinted there were things, secrets that Augustine knew ...'

Her brother is looking at her now. His eyes are quite dry, but the expression in them stirs her. He is all she has now, apart from Seth, and Seth is more his father's. More his own person, actually. She had been wrong about Seth, like she had been wrong about Martin. He had said to her, just now, 'I thought about you for a long time. But I am a weak man, Roxane.' She had not asked for that, and she still did not know what to make of it. But she knew he did not want her back. He had made that quite clear, when he said his life was new now, that he did not make deals with the past.

The thought of it made her bite her lips, and say to her brother on a rush of terror and love, 'Julius, there was a child. A child who is now an adult. A child who was brought up to remember all those things, who was schooled patiently by Mary, who waited, waited until the right moment. A child not mad, not incapably mad, like Mary, but made implacable by it all.'

There had been a child, he remembered that now. But he couldn't see the face, the eyes. All he could remember was the silent presence. 'So it was Mary's son, behind it all?' His voice is toneless now, he cannot absorb too much more. Roxane just looks at him, unable to speak for a moment. And in their eyes, in their faces, he sees what he cannot put into words, and the pain of it, the horror, the release sings through his veins with piercing clarity. And then Roxane speaks at last.

'Not a son, Julius. A daughter. Josie. Josephine Charlotte Cosgrove. A peculiar child, Martin said. A child who was forever dressing up, pretending she was someone else, a child disconnected from herself, but bright, a talented musician, and dangerous ... As you said, someone whose madness was more absence than presence. She had always been more her mother's child than his, in fact Marie kept saying how like her brother Lucien Josie was. After her mother died, he tried to get close to her, but he couldn't, she just ignored him completely. Martin said she'd become estranged from him, he hadn't seen her for a long time.' She stopped, something catching in her throat, the things Martin had told her, things she couldn't tell Julius yet, things she might never be able to tell him.

The child, head so close to her mother, and the woman whispering, whispering, words that went on and on and on, words he never tried to pierce, because he was ashamed, ashamed he could not help, had written himself out of it; the child, with her eyes on him, watching him with a cold calculation that made him feel infinitely desolate, the child with the box of papers the mother had left, papers she had never let him see. The shrine to the brother in the bedroom he was never allowed to enter, but which he'd seen once, and been sick at the thought of it. And his wife, Marie, whom he had not loved enough, but who was already, perhaps, in a place of no return even when he met her. He could not excuse himself, but it had been hard, and even at times tiresomely, grotesquely funny. And he had not divorced her. He at least had not divorced her. But still Martin did not know, could not see, maybe was unable to see, or else he'd fall apart. How the child—his child, as well as hers—had become so.

'She loved her mother,' he'd said, 'so much. And yet, at times, I felt it was almost like hate. They were completely eaten up with each other, so that when Marie died, it would have been an act of the grossest disloyalty for my daughter to have changed her mind about the Newtons. She couldn't; for in doing that, she would have had to stare into the abyss, into nothing. I suppose, in the end, if things are as you say, it was the hatred of Julius that kept my wife alive as long as she was. Not the love of our child. And I cannot believe that Josie would not have known that. Yet you understand also that it was that hatred which meant Marie herself could not destroy him, for then there would have been nothing ...'

There is nothing to be said now, nothing that can be said. There will have to be further, later, explanations, accomodations, living with the intolerable. But then the phone rings. No-one goes to it. Then as the tone clamours to a stop, and the answering machine clicks into life, they all hear the cold voice, relentlessly patient, polite: 'Good evening, Dr Newton, this is Charles Joseph Pym. Charles Joseph *Pym*. I have something here you might want to see again, Dr Newton, something I am sure you will want to see. A letter, yes, Dr Newton, in a hand you may know. It begins, "My dear*est* Lucien ..." Do you recognise it, Dr Newton? Shall I read it to you? Shall I, Dr Newton, just before I give it to Mr Tom Rice? This is not the end, you see, Dr Newton. Not the end at all. You see, Dr Newton, I will never let you go now. I will be waiting for you, Dr Newton. Always waiting.'

The darkness had materially increased, relieved only by the glare of the water thrown back from the white curtain before us. Many gigantic and pallidly white birds flew continuously now from beyond the veil, and their scream was the eternal 'Tekeli-li!' as they retreated from our vision. Hereupon Nu-Nu stirred in the bottom of the boat; but upon touching him, we found his spirit departed. And now we rushed into the embraces of the cataract, where a chasm threw itself open to receive us. But there arose in our pathway a shrouded human figure, very far larger in its proportions than any dweller among men. And the hue of the skin of the figure was of the perfect whiteness of the snow.

The Narrative of Arthur Gordon Pym
by Edgar Allen Poe

acknowledgments

I would like to publicly acknowledge the many people who helped me with their comments and encouragement at various stages in the writing of this book. In particular, I want to thank my husband, David Leach, for his loving patience and creative readings of the many drafts *The Hoax* went through; my agent, Margaret Connolly, for her unstintingly cheerful support; Belinda and Jennifer Byrne, for their instinctive belief in a difficult project; and to Amanda O'Connell for her editing.

Many thanks also to Christopher Koch for the generous and frank comments which helped me to cut the Gordian knot.

And last but certainly not least, many thanks go to my sister, Dominique Masson, and brother-in-law, the Australian composer Christopher Connolly. Thank you, Chris, for your invaluable advice on musical composition and the research material you so patiently collated and discussed with me. And for your inspirational setting of 'L'Albatros'. Thanks. I couldn't have done it without you.

bibliography

Although this book is a work of fiction, I read many books in the long process of writing it, and list these now for any interested readers.

PRIMARY

Baudelaire, Charles, *Les Fleurs du Mal*, Librairie Gründ, Paris.

Lennon, Peter, 'A Haydn to Nothing', (an article on the Haydn hoax), the *Guardian Weekly*, London and Sydney, January 16, 1994.

L'Illustration (magazine) Paris World Fair number, Paris 1890.

Marnat, Marcel, *Maurice Ravel*, Fayard, Paris 1988.

Poe, Edgar Allan, *Arthur Gordon Pym and Related Tales*, Oxford University Press, Oxford 1994.

——*Edgar Allan Poe: Essays and Reviews*, The Library of America, New York 1984.

Revue Musicale, 'Hommage à Maurice Ravel', Paris December 1938.

SACEM, *Le Centenaire de Maurice Ravel*, Paris 1975.

SECONDARY

Baudelaire, Charles, *Oeuvres Complètes,* ed. Y.G. Le Dantec, Gallimard, Paris 1963.

——*Selected Writing on Art and Artists,* translated and introduced by P.E. Charvet, Penguin, London 1972.

Campbell, Killis, *The Mind of Poe and Other Studies,* Russell and Russell, New York 1962.

Cooper, Barry, *Beethoven and the Creative Process,* Clarendon Press, Oxford 1990.

Davies, John Booth, *The Psychology of Music,* Hutchinson, London 1978.

Jansson, Tove, *Moominpappa at Sea,* Puffin, London 1966.

Kemp, Anthony E., *The Musical Temperament: Psychology and Personality in Musicians,* Oxford University Press, Oxford 1996.

Kopley, Richard (ed), *Poe's Pym: Critical Explorations,* Duke University Press, Durham and London 1992.

Leakey, F.W., *Baudelaire and Nature,* Manchester University Press, Manchester 1969.

Myers, Rollo H., *Ravel: Life and Work,* Gerald Duckworth and Co, London 1960.

Newman, William, *The Sonata since Beethoven,* University of North Carolina Press, Chapel Hill 1969.

Nichols, Roger, *Ravel,* JM Dent and Sons, London 1977.

——*Ravel Remembered,* Faber and Faber, London 1987.

Orenstein, Arbie (comp.and ed.) *A Ravel Reader: Correspondence, Articles, Interviews,* Columbia University Press, New York 1990.

Sonneck, O.G. (ed) *Beethoven: Impressions by his Contemporaries,* Dover, New York 1967.

Storr, Anthony, *Music and the Mind,* HarperCollins, London 1993.